DECEPT

BY

David Dowson

www.daviddowson.co.uk

Acknowledgements

To my mother, Beryl, who is always there for me, and my sister, Jan Webber, author of the Betty Illustrated children's books.

All rights reserved.

No part of this publication may be reproduced or stored in the retrieval system or transmitted, in any form, without the author's prior permission.

This book may not be reproduced in whole or in any form. Electronic or mechanical, including virtual copying, recording, or by any information storage and retrieval system now known or the hereafter invented without permission of the author.

Edition one

Copyright © David Dowson 2023

www.daviddowson.com

www.daviddowson.co.uk

Also, David Dowson

- Chess for Beginners
- Chess for Beginners Edition2
- Into the Realm of Chess
- Calculation
- Nursery Rhymes
- The Path of a Chess Amateur
- CHESS: The BeginnersCourse, Book:
- DECLON FIVE
- Dangers within
- The Murder of Inspector Hine
- DECEPTION

TABLE OF CONTENTS

CHAPTER ONE: A BRIEF HISTORY

Daniels's marriage to Anna Carter is a union that surprised and puzzled many due to the stark contrast in their appearances and backgrounds. Anna, a woman of beauty and social standing, described Daniel as ordinary and unremarkable. During their brief marriage, Anna discovered there was more to Daniel than meets the eye. He was a man of quiet disposition, often seen in ill-fitting and unflattering clothes. His physical appearance seemed incongruous with Anna's elegance and charm. The mismatched couple became a subject of gossip and intrigue among their social circles.

After only two years of marriage, Anna left Daniel for a Russian defector adding to their relationship's mystery. Her enigmatic statement about leaving him at the right time sparked curiosity and speculation among their acquaintances .BARON DACEY , a witness to their wedding, humorously remarked that Anna had married a RAT WITH SPECTCALES, highlighting the apparent disparity between the couple.

The contrasting personas and unexpected events in Daniel's life fascinated those who knew him. People questioned his origins, his wealth or lack thereof, and his occupation. The gossip mill tried to assign him a role, labelling him as either rich or poor, peasant or priest, to fit him into neat categorisations.

However, Daniel's true nature remained elusive, and his complexity defied simplistic characterisations. His unassuming appearance hid a sharp intellect and a dedication to his profession as an intelligence officer. Daniel's qualities and abilities went far beyond his outward appearance, challenging the shallow judgments of society.

Despite the end of his marriage and society's judgement, Daniel found solace and purpose in his work, immersing himself in the mysterious world of intelligence. In espionage, where truth and deception intertwine, Daniel thrived. His keen observational skills, analytical mind, and ability to unravel the mysteries of human behaviour set him apart.

The denial journey was one of contradictions, resilience, and the pursuit of truth amid a sea of lies. He had envisioned himself immersed in the literary obscurities of seventeenth-century Germany, devoting his days to research and contemplation. The tale of his life, filled with secrets, betrayals, and unexpected twists, would leave an indelible mark on the history of espionage, solidifying his place as one of its most intriguing and enigmatic figures of a life of intellectual pursuits and scholarly achievements. However, fate had other plans for Daniel. His tutor steered him from academic honours, leading him down a different path, gently drawn into intelligence work, a realm of secrets and hidden motives. It was a stark departure from his original aspirations but piqued his curiosity and offered him a new sense of purpose.

As Daniel's personal life took unexpected turns, such as his marriage to Anna and her subsequent departure, his dedication to his profession remained steadfast. He became engrossed in the intricacies of his work, finding solace and satisfaction in the intellectual challenges it presented. He delved into the mysteries of human behaviour, applying his astute deductions to decipher the enigmatic motives of individuals and unravel the intricate webs of espionage. With his fleshy face and bespectacled gaze, Daniel's appearance belied the complexities of his character and the depth of his knowledge.While Daniel's path had diverged from his initial dreams, he discovered a new form of fulfilment in his profession. The world of intelligence became his academic pursuit, offering him intellectual stimulation and the opportunity to make a meaningful impact. It was a life he embraced, surrounded by colleagues who shared his dedication and operated in the shadows alongside him. Daniel's journey, marked by unexpected twists and the constant interplay of love, loss, and duty, forged a resilient and enigmatic character. He embodied the juxtaposition of the intellectual and the clandestine, finding purpose in pursuing truth amid a world of deception.Daniel's Story would ultimately be one of sacrifice, resilience, and an unyielding dedication to his craft. His unassuming exterior concealed a keen intellect and unwavering determination, making him a formidable force in intelligence. And as he continued to navigate the complexities of his profession, Daniel left an indelible mark on the annals of espionage, forever entwined with the mysterious world he had chosen to inhabit and could not quite shake off the bewilderment of the day's events. As he sat in the darkened theatre, his mind wandered, replaying the interview and the tempting offer presented to him.The notion of working for the Secret Service intrigued Daniel. It appealed to his intellect and sense of adventure. It was a world of secrets, hidden motives, and undercover operations. Yet, it was also a world that carried significant risks and demanded unwavering loyalty. Daniel pondered the implications of such a path, considering its impact on his life and his pursuit of scholarly endeavours.The stage play blurred into a background hum as his thoughts consumed him. The chance to delve into the depths of human behaviour, to unravel mysteries and navigate the complex web of international intrigue, was undeniably tempting. He imagined the possibilities that lay before him if he accepted the offer. But some reservations gnawed at Daniel's conscience. He had always envisioned a life devoted to academia, immersed in the study of seventeenth-century Germany. Pursuing knowledge and its solitude had been his refuge, and he cherished the world of literary obscurities he had carved out for himself. However, the prospect of leaving behind the familiar and stepping into the unknown weighed heavily on Daniel. He considered the sacrifices he would have to make—abandoning his research, severing ties with his scholarly community, and embracing a life of secrecy and danger.

Daniel remained lost as the curtain fell while the audience applauded. The decision he faced was momentous, shaping the course of his life. It was a choice between the safety and comfort of his academic aspirations or the thrilling and treacherous path of espionage.With a heavy sigh, Daniel realised that fate was calling him to embark on a different journey that would test his intellect, courage, and loyalty. The allure of the

Secret Service proved too strong to resist, and he knew deep down that he could not turn his back on this opportunity. As he left the theatre, his mind was made up. Daniel would accept the offer, ready to embrace the challenges and uncertainties that awaited him. The life he had meticulously crafted would have to be set aside, and a new chapter would begin, leading him down a shadowy path where truth and deception intertwined. Little did Daniel know that his decision would set in motion a series of events that would shape the world of espionage and bring him face to face with a cunning adversary, testing his wit and resilience in ways he could never have imagined. Although he found solace in solitude and the prospect of working alone, the idea of being an anonymous instructor and engaging in frequent travel became more enticing. It offered him the fantastic prospect of independence and the ability to operate without direct contact or supervision. His first operational posting, a one-year appointment as a lecturer at the St Petersburg Provincial Russian University, provided a pleasant experience. He delivered lectures on Lord Byron to Russian students and spent vacations with them in hunting lodges. Among these students, he discreetly identified potential candidates he believed would be suitable for covert operations. He secretly passed his recommendations to an address in Bonn, unsure whether they would be accepted or ignored. He had no means of knowing if his messages ever reached their destination or if his candidates were ever approached. During his time in England, he had no contact with the Department he worked for, further adding to the air of secrecy.

Daniel's emotions regarding this work were conflicting and irreconcilable. On the one hand, he found it intriguing to assess and evaluate individuals' "agent potential" from a detached perspective. He devised small tests of character and behaviour to discern the qualities of a candidate. This part of him, acting as an international mercenary within his profession, lacked moral considerations and pursued personal gratification. On the other hand, he felt a sense of sadness as he witnessed the gradual decline of his ability to experience natural pleasure. Always withdrawn by nature, he increasingly found solace in his own company and the prospect of working independently, which further distanced him from the joys of ordinary life.He was shrinking from the temptations of friendship and human loyalty; he guarded himself warily from a spontaneous reaction. By the strength of his intellect, he forced himself to observe humanity with clinical objectivity. Because he was neither immortal nor infallible, he hated and feared the falseness of his life.But Daniel was a sentimental man and the long exile strengthened his deep love of England. He fed hungrily on memories of Cambridge, its beauty, its rational ease, and the mature slowness of its judgements. He dreamt of windswept autumn holidays at Hartland Quay, long trudges over the Cornish cliffs, his face smooth and hot against the sea wind. This was his other secret life, and he grew to hate the bawdy intrusion of the new Germany, the stamping and shouting of uniformed students, the scarred, arrogant faces, and their cheapjack answers. He resented, too, how the faculty

had tampered with his subject - his beloved German literature. There had been a terrible night in the winter of 1937 when Daniel had stood at his window and watched a great bonfire in the university court. Around the fire stood hundreds of students, their faces exultant and glistening in the dancing light. And into the pagan fire, they threw books in their hundreds. He knew whose books they were Thomas Mann, Heine, Lessing, and many others. Daniel's damp hand cupped around the end of his cigarette, watching and hating, triumphed that he knew his enemy.Nineteen thirty-nine saw him in Sweden, the accredited agent of a well-known Swiss small-arms manufacturer, his association with the firm conveniently backdated. Conveniently, his appearance had somehow altered, for Daniel had discovered a talent for the part that went beyond his hair's rudimentary change. He had played the part for four years, travelling between Poland, Hungary and Russia. He never guesses. It was impossible to be frightened for so long. Soon, he develops a nervous twitch. Left eye, it remained for 15 years later. He learns never to sleep, relax, or be at any time of the day or night. Against this background, he conducted his authentic commerce and his work as a spy. With time, his network grew, and other countries repaired their lack of foresight and preparation. In 1943 he was recalled within six weeks. He was yearning to return. But they never let him go. 'You're finished,' Steed-Asprey said: 'train new men, take time off. Get married or something. Unwind.' The war was over. Anna and Daniel would now be involved in a new war. The cold war created a demand for men of Daniel's experience. Daniel and Anna went to Cambridge for a small, deserved break. Daniel was ideal promotional material, and it dawned on him gradually that he had entered middle age without ever being Daniel and was - in the most excellent conceivable way - on the shelf. The job was new, the threat elusive, and he first enjoyed it. But younger men were coming in with fresher minds.

Things soon changed. Ivan Khrochny was gone. He fled from the new world to India, searching for another civilization. He died searching. He had boarded a train at Lille in 1941 with his radío operator, a native Belgian, and neither had been heard of again. Only Crawford remained, Crawford the professional, the war-time recruitment handler, the Ministers' Adviser on Intelligence; 'the first man,' had said, 'to play power tennis at Wimbledon.' The NATO alliance and the desperate measures the Americans contemplated altered the whole nature of Daniel's Service. Gone forever were the days of Steed-Asprey, when you took your orders over a glass of port in his rooms at Magdalen; the inspired amateurism of a handful of highly qualified, under-paid men had given way to the efficiency, bureaucracy and intrigue of a large Government department - effectively at the mercy of Crawford, with his expensive clothes and his knighthood, his distinguished grey hair and silver-coloured ties; Crawford, who even remembered his secretary's birthday, whose manners were a by-word among the ladies of the registry; Crawford, apologetically extending his empire and regretfully moving to even larger offices; Crawford, holding smart house-parties at Henley and feeding on the success of his subordinates ideas. The ideas they had brought him in during the war, the professional civil servant from an orthodox department, a man to handle paper and integrate the brilliance of his staff with the cumbersome machine of bureaucracy. It comforted the Great to deal with a man they knew who could reduce any colour to grey, who knew his masters and could walk among them. And he did it so well. They liked his shyness when he apologized for the company he kept, his insincerity when he defended the vagaries of his subordinates, and his flexibility when formulating.

Daniel rose from his seat in the theatre and made for the exit. He flagged down a taxi and walked in. As Daniel sat in the back of a London taxi on Wednesday, 4 January, he reflected on his current situation. Over the years, he had acquired numerous advantages and commitments, such as his new dagger, Asprey Service position, and role as a minister's adviser. Despite these achievements, he could not help but feel a sense of nostalgia and longing for his humble beginnings in a dilapidated terrace house in Knightsbridge. The contrast between his status and past seemed to manifest physically, as he appeared hunched and frog-like, earning him the nickname 'Mole' among his colleagues. However, his secretary, Mary, held him in high regard, affectionately referring to him as "My darling teddy bear."

Due to his age and the toll his previous endeavours took during the war, Crawford advised Daniel that he was now too old to go abroad. It was suggested that he should remain at home and tend to his responsibilities there, symbolized by the metaphorical notion of "keeping the home fires burning."

CHAPTER TWO

In the early hours of 5 January, Daniel found himself on his way to Cambridge Craft. The reason for his journey is yet to be revealed. Daniel slid into his chair, his nerves involuntarily relaxed. He felt cosy like he was wrapped in the comforting cocoon of his soft, warm blankets. Outside, the rain fell gently, casting a hazy mist over the world beyond his window. The evening was shrouded in a dream-like ambience, an ethereal calm that permeated the air. As Daniel sank further into the embrace of his bed, a surreal sense of tranquillity washed over him. He felt weightless as if floating on a cloud, his mind adrift in a realm where reality and imagination intertwined. The raindrops tapping against the glass became a delicate symphony, lulling him into profound relaxation.

An inexplicable chill enveloped the room, causing goosebumps to ripple across Daniel's skin. Yet, instead of fear, he found himself inexplicably drawn to the ghostly presence. It beckoned to him, an enigmatic invitation into the unknown.

With cautious curiosity, Daniel ventured into the spectral realm. Reality melted away, and he drifted through a kaleidoscope of swirling colors and abstract shapes. The boundaries of time and space dissolved, leaving him adrift in a realm governed by his subconscious.

Daniel soon blinked himself out of his dreams to the streets of London that flew past him as the Taxi zoomed on. Thoughts swirled through his mind as he pondered the enigma before him. Unlike other capitals, London seemed to lose its distinct character at night. The vibrant streets transformed into dimly lit alleys, where the hum of activity dwindled and a sense of mystery took hold. Daniel wondered if the shifting shadows or the subdued atmosphere cloaked the city, erasing its daytime vibrancy. Lost in contemplation, he quietly longed to uncover the secrets London's nighttime facade concealed, yearning to glimpse its hidden allure.

As the taxi turned onto the road leading to the Factory, Daniel suddenly sat upright, startled. The reason for the Duty Officer's call came rushing back to him, abruptly pulling him out of his dreams and wishes. The details of their conversation flooded back into his mind, as if his memory had perfected the art of recollection through years of practice.

"I have the Adviser on the line," the Duty Officer had said, addressing Daniel by name. 'Daniel; it's Mason speaking. You interviewed Samuel Arthur at the Foreign Office on Monday, am I right?'

Daniel responded to the Duty Officer, confirming that he did recall the conversation. "The case," Daniel continued, "was a routine anonymous interview. A letter, authorized by the Party, alleged that the Director had ties to Security. It happened at Cambridge."

Daniel silently reassured himself, "Finnan can't have complained. I would have cleared him. There was nothing irregular, nothing."

The Duty Officer's concern was evident in his next question, "Did you confront him? Was it hostile, Daniel? Tell me."

Daniel sensed the fear in the Duty Officer's voice, realizing that Finnan must have brought the entire Cabinet into the situation. He replied, "No, it was actually a very friendly interview. We got along well. In fact, I went beyond the scope of my assignment,' Daniel explained further, responding to the Duty Officer's inquiry, "Well, I more or less reassured him. I told him not to worry."

The Duty Officer expressed surprise, "You what?" Daniel clarified, "I told him not to worry. He was obviously distressed, and so I reassured him."

Curious, the Duty Officer asked, "What exactly did you tell him?"

"I said that I, as well as the Service, had no authority or reason to trouble him any further," Daniel replied.

The Duty Officer inquired, "Is that all?"

Daniel confirmed, "Yes, that's all I told him..."ay."

Daniel paused for a second; he had never known Mason like this or him so dependent. 'Yes, that's all. Absolutely all.' He'll never forgive me for this. So much for the studied calm, the cream shirts and silver ties, the smart luncheons with Ministers, Daniel thought.

'He says you cast doubts on his loyalty, that his car in the F is ruined, that he is the victim of paid informers.'

'He said what? He must have gone stark mad. He knows he's cleared. What else does he want?'

'Nothing. He's dead. Killed himself at 8:30 this evening. Left a letter to the Foreign Secretary. The police rang one of his secretaries and got permission to open the letter. Then they told us. There's going to be an inquiry. Daniel, you're sure, aren't you?'

'Sure of what?'

'... Never mind. Get round as soon as you can.'

It had taken him hours to get a taxi. He rang three cab ranks and got no reply. At last, the Sloane Square rank replied, and Daniel waited at his bedroom window wrapped in his overcoat until he saw the cab draw up at the door. It reminded him of the air raids in Germany, this unreal anxiety in the dead of night.

At Cambridge Factory, he stopped the cab a hundred yards from the office, partly from habit and partly to clear his head in anticipation of Mason's febrile questioning.

He showed his pass to the constable on duty and made his way slowly to the lift. The Duty Officer greeted him with relief as he emerged, and they walked together down the bright cream corridor.

Mason had gone to Scotland Yard to meet with Sparrow. There was a disagreement regarding which police department should handle the case. Sparrow believed it should be the Special Branch, while Evelyn argued for CID involvement. Additionally, the Surrey police needed to be informed about the situation.

Daniel suggested, "Let's go and have coffee in the Duty Officer's office. It may not be the best quality, but it's available." Daniel felt relieved that it was Peter Gillam on duty that night. Peter was a polished and thoughtful man, with expertise in satellite espionage. He was always well-prepared with a timetable and a penknife, embodying a friendly and helpful demeanor.

Meanwhile, Finnan's wife had gone to the theatre but returned alone around a quarter to eleven. She eventually contacted the police, and they found Finnan's body at twelve-five in the morning. It was revealed that he resided somewhere in Surrey.

Later in the day, In the Metropolitan Watson area, near the Secretary's office on the Kingston by-pass, Day's body was found outside. The superintendent at the Foreign-Home office contacted the Graham, Chief Constable, who reached out to the Duty Officer. The Chief Constable referred to the Foreign Office as the "Goon."

The Director of Personnel at the Foreign Office had called, requesting the Adviser's home number. He expressed frustration, stating that Security had interfered with his staff for the last time. He believed Day had been a loyal and talented officer, criticizing Security for using Gestapo-like methods without a genuine threat.

The Duty Officer handled the call, providing the Director of Personnel with the Adviser's number. Meanwhile, the Duty Officer dialed Mason on another line to inform him of the news. This occurred at around twelve-twenty. By one o'clock, Mason arrived with Daniel, in a highly agitated state. He would need to report to the Minister the next morning.

For a moment, there was silence as Graham poured coffee essence into the cups and added boiling water from the electric kettle. Curious, Graham asked, "What was Day like?"

Daniel responded, "Until tonight, I could have given you a detailed description. But now, he seems to require more understanding. In terms of appearance, he was obviously Jewish. He came from an Orthodox family but abandoned those traditions at Oxford and became a Marxist. He was perceptive, cultured, and a reasonable man. Soft-spoken and a good listener. He had a thorough education, with a wealth of knowledge. However, whoever denounced him was correct; he was a member of the Party."

"How old was Day?" Graham asked

"Forty-four," Daniel replied. "Although he looked older, to be honest. He had a sensitive face, with a mop of straight dark hair in the fashion of an undergraduate. His profile resembled that of a twenty-year-old, with delicate, dry skin that had a somewhat chalky appearance. His face was heavily lined, with lines going in various directions, almost like a grid. He had skinny fingers and was a compact individual—a self-contained unit. He seemed to enjoy his pleasures in solitude and also suffered alone."

Daniel and Mason soon went back to Mason's office. Mason left briefly to attend to somethings outside and reentered again. He greeted Daniel, patting him on the shoulder with his left arm. Mason's office had no government property; instead, he had adorned the walls with nineteenth-century watercolors that he had purchased. The rest of the room seemed ordinary and off-the-shelf, according to Daniel's observation. Mason himself seemed to fit that description as well. His suit was a bit too light for proper respectability, the string of his monocle crossing his cream shirt as usual. He wore a light grey woolen tie. Daniel thought a German would describe him as "flott" or chic—a barmaid's dream of a real gentleman.

Mason provided an update, saying, "I've seen Sparrow. It's clearly a case of suicide. The body has been removed, and the Chief Constable won't act beyond the standard procedures. An inquest will be held in a day or two. It has been agreed upon— and I cannot stress this enough, Daniel— that our previous interest in Day should not be mentioned to the press."

Daniel responded, "I see." You're dangerous, Mason. You're weak and frightened. You'd sacrifice anyone to save yourself. I can see it in the way you look at me—evaluating me for potential harm, Daniel thought

"Don't think I'm criticizing, Daniel. If the Director of Security authorized the interview, you have nothing to worry about," Mason added.

"Quite right, except for one thing, Mason," Daniel replied, suggesting unfortunate implications. "The Director of Security authorized the interview. He omitted it from your minute but verbally confirmed it. I'm not sure if he'll have any doubts about it, but he can confirm if needed."

Daniel seemed uncompromising, his gaze shifting towards Mason's stick once again. Mason, on the other hand, appeared sharp and calculating. He wanted Daniel to conspire with him.

"Day's office has been in touch with me," Mason continued.

"Yes," Daniel acknowledged.

"There will inevitably be an inquiry, and it may be impossible to keep the press out. You won't scare me and get me to cooperate... I'm getting closer to retirement, and I have my own considerations... I'm unemployable but won't participate in your deception, Mason. I will have to meet with the Home Secretary first thing tomorrow," Mason stated, subtly attempting to instill fear in Daniel and manipulate him.

"I must have all the facts, Daniel. I must do my duty," Mason insisted. "If there's anything you haven't recorded or haven't told me about that interview, please inform me now, and I will judge its significance."

Daniel responded firmly, "There's nothing to add to what's already in the file and what I told you earlier tonight. However, it might be helpful for you to know that I conducted the interview in an exceptionally informal atmosphere. The allegation against Day was weak—his university membership in the thirties and vague talk of current sympathies. Half the Cabinet was in the Party in the thirties."

Mason frowned, while Daniel continued "When I arrived at Day's room at the Foreign Office, he seemed to have spent the whole time preparing to go out. He suggested that we should stroll to the park."

"Goon," Daniel muttered under his breath. "Well, we did. It was a sunny but cold day, rather pleasant. We watched the ducks," Daniel replied. Mason showed impatience with his gesture. "We spent about half an hour in the park, with him doing most of the talking. Day was an intelligent man, fluent and engaging. However, he was naturally nervous too. People like him often enjoy talking about themselves, and I think he was relieved to get it off his chest. He told me the whole story and didn't hesitate to mention names. Afterward, we went to an espresso cafe he knew near Millbank."

"An espresso bar?" Mason questioned.

"Yes, they sell a special kind of coffee for a shilling. We had some," Daniel explained.

"I see. So, it was under these... convivial circumstances that you informed him that the Department would recommend no action," Mason stated.

"Yes, it's something we often do, although we don't usually record it," Daniel confirmed. He noticed Mason nodding, understanding this aspect of the situation. Daniel thought to himself, Goodness me, he really is quite pitiful. It's rather satisfying to see Mason being as unpleasant as I expected.

"And may I assume, therefore, that his suicide—and his letter, of course—came as a complete surprise to you? You have no explanation?" Mason inquired.

"It would be quite remarkable if I did," Daniel responded.

"Do you have any idea who might have denounced him?" Mason continued.

"No," Daniel replied simply.

"He was married, you know," Mason mentioned.

"Yes," Daniel acknowledged.

"I wonder... His wife might be able to provide some insights. I hesitate to suggest it, but someone from the Department should speak to her and inquire further, within the bounds of sensitivity," Mason proposed.

"Now?" Daniel looked at Mason with an expressionless face.

Mason stood behind his desk, his whole demeanor exuding an air of professionalism. Daniel observed the businessman-like appearance of Mason, admiring his pristine white cuffs and the cutlery set arranged neatly on his desk.

Mason toyed with a large flat cigarette box, showing his full hands.

Mason looked up, his face displaying sympathy. "Daniel, I understand the emotions you must be experiencing, but despite this tragic event, you must try to comprehend the situation. Any information regarding Day's state of mind immediately after his interview with us, including whether he spoke to his wife about it, is crucial for our understanding. The Minister and the Home Secretary will demand a comprehensive account of this affair, and I am responsible for providing one. Although it is not officially sanctioned, we must be realistic."

"Do you want me to go and speak to her?" Daniel asked.

"Someone must. The inquest is pending, and the Home Secretary will have to decide. We still need the facts, and time is short. You are familiar with the case and have conducted background inquiries. There is no time for anyone else to familiarize themselves with the details. If anyone is to go, it has to be you, Daniel."

"When do you want me to go?" Daniel inquired.

"Apparently, Mrs. Day is quite a conventional woman. She is of foreign origin and, I believe, Jewish. She suffered greatly during the war, which adds to the situation's complexity. However, she is strong-minded and appears unaffected by her husband's death, at least superficially. But she is sensible and willing to communicate. Sparrow informed me that she is being cooperative. The Surrey police can be notified of your visit, and you can meet with her first thing in the morning. I will contact you there later in the day."

Daniel turned to leave, but Mason's hand on his arm stopped him. He turned back to face Mason, who wore a smile typically reserved for older women in the Service.

"Daniel, you can rely on me, you know. You can count on my support," Mason assured him.

As Daniel walked out onto the street, he couldn't help but think, "My God, you truly work tirelessly. You're like a 24-hour cabaret. 'We Never Close'."

CHAPTER THREE

The morning of the next day, Daniel walked down the streets of London. As usual, he stopped the taxi, a hundred yards from his destination to clear his head. Something weighted heavily on his shoulders. He wasn't sure what it was. It was impossible for him to feel guilt, perhaps it was sadness. Sadness for Day and his deceased wife. That sounds more likely. As he walked on in the street the thought of moments he had as and enjoyed in espionage filled him with equal amounts of guilt and pleasure, considering Finnan had killed himself for such a reason. Here he was, he had left that life behind like the Brutalist London building he walked past. First it was Finnan, now Day.

Finnan had his justified reason, he was found out, but Day? Why Day?

Daniel steady his steps on the street, surrounded by the silence of the middle class London neighborhood street. The stillness seemed to amplify the restlessness within his mind, as he grappled with the weight of his solitude. Daniel's thoughts twisted and turned, spiraling down a labyrinthine path. He pondered the nature of guilt, its insidious grip on his consciousness. Memories of his covert past as a spy resurfaced, haunting him like specters from another lifetime. The shadows of his clandestine actions danced before his eyes, flickering reminders of his choices and the lives he had affected. Why now? Was it grief that got him this way or age?

A sense of restlessness consumed him, a gnawing unease that grew more potent with each step he took. ‘I'm getting too old of this.’ he muttered. As Daniel soaked in the beauty and the serenity of the London streets on the outside and battled the spirals of emotions on the inside. He wondered if his actions had been justified, if the pursuit of a greater cause had truly outweighed the moral compromises he had made. Were the secrets he had guarded worth their toll on his soul? Doubt seeped into his every thought, infiltrating the very core of his being. He, amid blissful solitude. He found that loneliness became a canvas upon which his thoughts painted vivid scenes of missed connections and lost opportunities. Strangely, in that moment, he questioned why he had chosen a life of isolation, a path that had left him adrift, disconnected from the world around him. Was it the consequence of his choices, or had he always been destined to wander this desolate path alone?

Daniel's mind became a battleground of introspection, fighting against the heavy burden of regret of the missed connections and the lost opportunities. He yearned for some sort of redemption, or maybe a release from these emotions. Perhaps a chance to find peace within himself, though he'll not likely find it anytime soon. But until that elusive day arrived, he would remain trapped in the labyrinth of his thoughts, grappling with guilt, restlessness, and the echoes of a life lived on the edge. Still, amid his internal turmoil, he sorts the darkness and the solace the darkness brings.

The memories of Day lingered and the last moment they shared together. It was a beautiful day. At least he could say that now that that moment was over. Day stood tall and vibrant, eyes alight with enthusiasm as he spoke animatedly. Daniel remembered how Day's words dashed through the air, vividly depicting his ideals and aspirations. It was a moment of pure authenticity, untainted by the complexities.

As Daniel reminisced, he lifted again, feeling the sun's warmth on his skin and hearing the rustle of leaves beneath their feet. The park had been a tranquil sanctuary amidst the bustling city, just like the streets he worked in. It was a temporary escape from the chaos that accompanied their clandestine lives. In that rare moment, Daniel could almost tell he was simultaneously at ease with himself and somebody else. Something that had only happened with Anna and his mother.

Daniel yearned for the taste of the espresso that they had shared. The aroma of freshly brewed coffee permeated the air, mingling with the soft chatter of other patrons. They had settled into a cozy corner, sipping their espressos as they continued their conversation.

Day's face had radiated joy and contentment, his eyes twinkling with excitement as he shared his dreams of a better world and his unwavering belief in the power of collective action. His passion was infectious. But Daniel was immune. At that moment, there was silence. It was as if they both communicated things they knew that they knew but didn't walk to talk about through the silence. To him, it was nothing too serious. But as he walked up to the white picket fence of Mrs. Day’s house he knew he should have thought better.

Mrs. Day's home is nestled in a quaint English neighborhood, it exuded an air of domestic tranquility and the charm of a bygone era. The house's exterior boasted a classic red brick facade, complemented by large windows adorned with delicate lace curtains. The white picket fence framed the front yard, adorned with blooming flowers that added a touch of color to the well-manicured lawn.

Daniel walked in through the fence and knocked on the door. It was interesting to see things still in order despite the grieving, Daniel thought. He knocked again and this time the door got opened by Mrs. Day. She looked surprised to see Daniel. 'Officer Daniel, hello.' she said... 'Hello Lydia.' Mrs. Day exuded a quiet grace that belied her unassuming appearance. Lines of grief etched delicate creases around her eyes and mouth. 'Do come in.' she left the door for Daniel and walked in.

Daniel stepped into the house, looking around the serene and clean atmosphere. The interior decor embodied the style of the time, embracing traditional and modern elements. The walls were adorned with floral wallpaper, gently reflecting the natural light that filtered through the windows.

The living room, adorned with plush floral sofas and an intricately patterned rug, offered Lydia and her children a cosy retreat. The room's focal point was a fireplace, framed by a polished wooden mantelpiece adorned with family photographs and delicate trinkets. A sense of nostalgia emanated from every corner, capturing the essence of a simpler time. Daniel walked up to the picture frames and saw a large portrait of Day on the wall amidst the other little portions of the family together.

'Excuse me Daniel, let me finish what I have going on in the kitchen.' Mrs. Day said and walked into the Kitchen. The kitchen, which looked to be the heart of Lydia's domain, was a testament to her culinary prowess. Pastel-colored cabinets lined the walls, housing an array of vintage utensils and colorful mixing bowls. A well-worn wooden dining table sat at the center of the room, surrounded by mismatched chairs, each with its own story. The kitchen window overlooked a well-tended backyard garden, where Lydia nurtured various herbs and vegetables.

A small study served as Lydia's private retreat in one corner of the house. The room housed an antique writing desk with handwritten notes and a well-worn diary. Bookshelves lined the walls, filled with classic novels and recipe books that Lydia cherished, a testament to her love of literature and homemaking.

Lydia's home was a sanctuary from the outside world, reflecting her dedication to creating a haven for her family. It was a place where cherished memories were made, where laughter and love intertwined with the gentle ticking of a vintage clock. A place where warmth, comfort, and a sense of tradition harmoniously coexisted. Though it all seems to be standing still now, Daniel knew it was all a facade. It was only a matter of time it all crumbled into chaos.

Lydia soon left the kitchen and cleaned her hands with a hand towel. Her hands, weathered by years of household chores and tending to her loved ones, revealed the marks of a life lived in service. Her complexion, fair with a hint of a rosy glow, spoke of days spent in the gentle embrace of the English sun, finding solace in the simple pleasures of gardening or leisurely walks in the park. Daniel remembered Lydia's face reflected joy and laughter. Though not conventionally striking, her features carried a certain charm and depth that captivated those who took the time to notice. With chestnut brown hair styled in a simple yet elegant bob. She possessed a softness that emanated from her warm hazel eyes. They sparkled with a mixture of warmth. It is all gone now. She looked tired, weary and sad despite trying to keep an upright and uptight appearance.

She walked to Daniel and sat across him, crossing her legs. Her modest dress, chosen with care to reflect her timeless elegance. Subtle floral patterns or delicate polka dots adorned the fabrics, adding a touch of femininity to her otherwise understated ensemble. She gave a wry smile afterwards that had sadness in it edges

Daniel observed her with keen eyes. 'I believe you're here to pay your last respects' Lydia said. Her voice carried a softness and gentleness, mirroring the

tenderness with which she cared for her loved ones. Daniel found this a little off character.
'No Lydia, I was told to come for some questions, regarding the investigation going on.'
Lydia's looked away avoiding eye contact. Knowing you guys are quite close, 'That must be tough.' Daniel nodded. 'He was quite happy in our last moments together. I would never have thought...'
Lydia nodded, blinking her eyes.
'And the children'
'They are off to school.' Lydia said, still looking away.

As the small talk continued, Daniel sat across from Lydia Day, observing her every move keenly. As she navigated through their conversation, he couldn't help but feel a sense of dissatisfaction. Her words danced around the edges of his enquiries, leaving him with little to grasp onto, and he could sense there was more she wasn't revealing.

The room was adorned with delicate decor, a facade of tranquility that belied the turmoil within. Lydia's eyes darted around the room, avoiding direct contact with Daniel. Her hands trembled slightly, betraying the nervousness that seeped into her every gesture.

Perhaps he wasn't the sharper guy for the job. But years of espionage had sharpened his observation. He understood the importance of observation, of paying attention to the smallest details. Lydia's body language spoke volumes, depicting unease and guardedness.

He watched as she tucked a strand of hair behind her ear, a subtle gesture that hinted at her desire to maintain control. Her shoulders tensed, a sign of the weight she carried on her fragile frame. She seemed restless, as if her mind was racing, contemplating what to share and conceal.

"Lydia," Daniel began, his voice calm yet persistent. "I know this is a difficult time for you, but it's crucial that we understand the events leading up to your husband's suicide. Every detail could be important in our investigation. Please, try to recall anything that might illuminate his mind."

Lydia fidgeted in her seat, a restless energy emanating from her. Her gaze shifted from Daniel to the floor, avoiding Daniel's probing eyes. She sighed, her voice tinged with frustration. "He didn't share much with me in those final days. He was just as happy has you met him"

Daniel's dissatisfaction grew, there was more beneath the surface, clear as day. This even made him more comfortable. It was easier if this was straightforward and they got everything over with. But with these hidden truths lurking in the background, Daniel restlessness resumed.

Sitting in his office, Daniel pondered the circumstances that made Mason to involve him. He leaned back in his chair and his thoughts swirled with uncertainty. Mason had always been a shrewd and calculating individual who played the game of intelligence with finesse. Though he was not always the smartest in the room. The fact that he had sought Daniel's involvement raised suspicion in his mind. This case could have gone to some else. Someone younger and vibrant for the tasking job ahead.

A sense of doubt crept into his thoughts. Was he using Daniel as a pawn in a larger scheme?
Was he being manipulated? Was Mason exploiting their shared history to draw him into a web of deceit and danger? Daniel couldn't ignore the nagging feeling that he was being used, that he had become a pawn in a game he didn't fully understand.

Still, Daniel felt invested already. Day was not a person he would necessarily call a friend but they went way back. He had his down times but was resilient and stood for his beliefs. Day constantly told him of his dreams of the future of England. To an extent Daniel participated in those dreams hoping one day it could be a reality. He had no reason to kill himself.

Daniel picked up the case file, poring over the details with a critical eye. His mind drifted to a moment when he was a little boy in Germany. He was always found playing with his neighborhood friends at the local park. They had all decided to play hide and seek when Daniel spotted Timmy sneaking behind a tree and taking a peek at the hiding spots of the other children. Timmy was known for his mischievous nature and clever tactics. But on this particular day. It was clear that Timmy was up to no good and trying to gain an unfair advantage in the game.

Unable to contain his sense of justice, Daniel decided to outsmart his mischievous friend. As Timmy continued to sneak around, Daniel devised a cunning plan. He discreetly signaled to the other children, urging them to quietly change their hiding spots while Timmy was preoccupied.

Timmy approached the next hiding spot and expected to find one of the other children. To his surprise, the spot was empty. Confused, he scratched his head and moved on to the next spot, only to find it empty. The other children had seamlessly moved, leaving Timmy in disbelief. With a twinkle in his eye, Daniel emerged from his hiding spot and confronted Timmy with a mischievous grin.

"Foul Play!" Daniel exclaimed, pointing an accusing finger at his cheating friend.

Timmy's face turned beet red as he realized his sneaky tactics had been discovered. He sheepishly admitted his attempt to cheat and apologized to the rest of the group. The other children couldn't help but burst into laughter, amused by the turn of events. It was funny to everyone else except Daniel. He had never expected such from Timmy because he viewed the world with the eyes of innocence. That moment took the veil of innocence off Daniel's eyes and plunged him into a world of deep introspection, suspension and SCEPTICISM.

That moment, doubt lingered, but so did determination. Daniel knew he couldn't abandon the investigation. He owes if not anyone but himself the truth. If Mason had ulterior motives, he would need to navigate the treacherous waters of deceit and manipulation to uncover the real story behind Day's suicide.

Daniel set aside his doubts and pushed forward. The restlessness grinded into a steely resolve, driving him more to inquisitiveness. He would tread carefully, mindful of the risks, and determined to navigate these truths that lurk in the shadows

CHAPTER FOUR

In the depths of the night, Daniel found himself standing amidst a sea of shadowy figures, their faces distorted and indistinguishable. He was paralyzed, unable to move or speak, as if trapped in a macabre theatre where he was both spectator and participant.

The shadows around him whispered unintelligible secrets, their voices mingling with the echoing screams of agony. A chorus of despair filled the air, each note a symphony of suffering. The weight of guilt and remorse bore down Daniel's shoulders, threatening to crush his spirit.

The dream materialized in a desolate, dimly lit alley, the air thick with tension and the stench of fear. Daniel stood amidst a sea of shadowy figures, their faces distorted and indistinguishable. He was paralyzed, unable to move or speak, as if trapped in a macabre theatre where he was both spectator and participant.

Blood seeped into every crevice of his consciousness, staining his hands crimson. The metallic scent of iron filled the air, assaulting his senses. He glanced down at his hands, shocked and repulsed by the sight of blood.

Faces emerged from the darkness, distorted and twisted by pain. The victims of his past, innocent lives caught in the crossfire of political games, stared at him with hollow eyes. Their pleading gazes bore into his soul, accusing him of betrayal, demanding justice. He shot his eyes tight, trying to wring himself off the subconscious world of horror.

In the chaos, he saw himself—no longer the passive observer, but an active participant in this nightmarish theatre. His body moved with an unnatural fluidity, his hands striking out, inflicting pain upon others. The dream distorted his identity, blurring the line between perpetrator and victim.

The dream offered no respite, no escape from the relentless cycle of violence. Every blow he delivered, every life he took, sent shockwaves of horror through his being. It was a twisted distortion of his reality, a grotesque manifestation of the consequences he never thought he deserved.

A sudden jolt shot him off this world of horror. He sat on his bed, awake. His body drenched in a cold sweat as his heart raced like a runaway train. He sat upright and held his chest tight. His mind reeling from the vivid and horrifying journey his dream had taken him on. The remnants of the dream clung to him like a shroud, haunting his every thought.

Like a character in his nightmare, restlessness resumed again. He rose from his bed and staggered in the darkness to his window, as if seeking solace in the million lights in the night sky.

As the million lights in the sky dissolved into a single one, the weight of the dream lingered like a heavy burden on his shoulders, as Daniel entered Mason brightly lit watercolor painted office.
He recounted his recent visit to Day's wife and his unsettling encounter with her agitation.

"She was visibly agitated when I asked about Day's last days. There's something she's not saying. So much for her been cooperative" he glared at Mason

Mason leaned back in his chair, 'Look, maybe you met her at the wrong time.' Mason scratched his temples "Maybe, Day's suicide seemed too straightforward, too neat. We need to dig deeper. The autopsy result should be out today" Mason seem distracted and concerned about something else. You're not thinking what I'm thinking Mason, are you? You're not trying to dig me deeper into this are you?

"'You're not getting me involved any further are you?'

Mason's hands reached to the tea pot on the table and poured it into his cup. He dropped the pot, reached out underneath his desk and threw a file at Daniel. 'The

Ministry agreed on this. It's not my doing.' He kept his eyes on the tea while avoiding Daniel's gaze.

Daniel grabbed the file and opened it. While Mason's lips curved into a knowing smile. "Daniel, there's a reason why you were chosen for this case. You have a unique insight, a personal connection to Day. Besides, you've already taken the initiative in speaking with Day's wife. Consider yourself the lead investigator."

The weight of the settled deeply on Daniel's shoulders, this time it was more of a burden that mingled with a sense of both duty mixed with a lot of uncertainty. After several long years trying to fight this here he was at the spot he avoided. He was drawn back into the murky world of secrets and deceit.

As he walked through the bustling corridors of the precinct, in resignation of this unexpected twist, Daniel's thoughts raced, Mason had always been a shrewd and ambitious detective, willing to cross ethical boundaries to achieve his desired outcomes. Knowing Mason had no hands in this, he could help but wonder what prompted the ministry on such a blind and vague decision.

As he settled on his office desk, the memory of his dream lingered in the recesses of his mind, reminding him of the darkness within him.

Mary, perceptive as always, noticed the furrowed lines on Daniel's forehead and approached him with concern in her eyes. Sensing his restlessness, she gently asked, "Is everything alright, Teddy bear? You seem troubled."

Daniel sighed, his gaze fixed on a distant point he looked at Mary's worried face and sighed. She would only keep insisting if he does open up. Plus, he is curious to know what a detached character though of the state of the swirling thoughts and emotions of his mind

"Mary," he began, his voice laced with exhaustion, "I had the most unsettling dream last night. It was unlike anything I've ever experienced before."

Mary looked up from her work, concern etched across her face. "What happened, Daniel? You can tell me. Sometimes sharing our fears can help alleviate their hold on us."

Daniel almost rolled his eye 'I'm not afraid, Mary. Just unsettled. Daniel recounted the dream, describing how he was immersed in a world of bloodshed and violence, despite hardly being involved in physical combat even during war. The dream portrayed him as a participant in gruesome acts, covered in the blood of others. The mere recollection sent shivers down his spine.

Daniel was hoping for a feeling of relief as he finished recounting the dream. Unlike most people this was not a period of vulnerability for him. It was a moment of wishing for a means to understand and to escape the reality he hoped wasn't coming up to catch up with him.
"You know, Daniel," Mary said softly, her eyes filled with a mixture of sympathy and curiosity, "there is an old superstition that dreams involving blood are a sign of impending death. Some believe that such dreams are an omen, a warning of tragedy or loss to come."

Daniel's brows furrowed in irritation... Her response caught him off guard. He had always valued Mary's companionship and appreciated her insights, but this time, her mention of superstition struck a nerve. He dismissed her words with a slight wave of his hand, his tone revealing his frustration.

"Superstitions, Mary? Really? You know I don't put much stock in such beliefs. Dreams are just the subconscious mind playing tricks on us. They don't hold any deeper meaning or foretell the future."
Daniel said and felt comfort in his explanation.
Mary nodded understandingly, sensing Daniel's irritation. "I apologize, Daniel. I didn't mean to upset you. I understand that you rely on logic and reason.

When Mary was done assisting she left for the day. Daniel sat alone in his office, waiting for the reports on Day's autopsy to arrive, she thought of what Mary said. Wasn't it quite convenient to cut off all logic and hard truths and swing onto fantasies and the falsies of life. He wondered if he won't be feeling the pain on his shoulders if he subscribe to those

His eyes grew heavy, Daniel found himself drifting into a familiar realm—a lucid dream that offered solace and respite from the shadows of his past. In this dreamscape, he was transported to a lecture hall, surrounded by eager students, their faces filled with curiosity and anticipation.

He stood at the podium, the scent of old books and the warm glow of knowledge filling the air. His lecture's topic was the renowned poet Lord Byron—a figure Daniel had long admired for his wit, rebellion, and romanticism. The excitement radiated from him as he delved into the intricacies of Byron's works, passionately dissecting the themes and shedding light on the poet's profound impact on literature.

As he spoke, Daniel felt a surge of pride and satisfaction. His students were engaged, hanging on to his every word. Their eyes sparkled with a thirst for knowledge, their faces reflecting a deep appreciation for the art of poetry. He reveled in their eagerness to learn, their hunger for understanding.

Each question posed by his students brought him joy, as it revealed their intellectual growth and the impact of his teachings. Daniel's heart swelled with a sense of accomplishment, knowing that he had made a difference in their lives, helping them navigate the complex labyrinth of literature.

Amid the lecture, a young woman raised her hand, her face brimming with curiosity.

Daniel recognized her as Maria, a particularly talented student who showed great promise in understanding Byron's works.

"Yes, Maria, please go ahead," Daniel encouraged, a gentle smile gracing his lips.

Maria's voice resonated earnestly as she asked, "Professor, what do you think Lord Byron would say about the modern world? Do you think his revolutionary spirit would find a place in our current society?"

Daniel's eyes lit up with excitement at the thought-provoking question. He delved into a captivating discourse, exploring the essence of Byron's spirit and its timeless relevance. As he shared his insights, a lively discussion unfolded, with students eagerly participating, their thoughts intertwining in a symphony of intellectual exchange.

In this dream realm, Daniel felt a sense of belonging, a purpose beyond the constraints of his investigative duties. He relished the opportunity to inspire young minds, to ignite their passion for literature, and to foster their critical thinking abilities.

Time seemed to lose its hold within the dream, and Daniel reveled in the endless possibilities that stretched before him. His lucid dreaming allowed him to explore new avenues of knowledge, to unlock the depths of his intellectual curiosity, and to experience moments of fulfilment and contentment.

But as the dream faded, reality seeped back into Daniel's consciousness. He knew he had to return to the investigation, to face the harsh truths that awaited him. The reports on Day's autopsy would soon arrive, bringing him one step closer to

unravelling the mysteries surrounding Day's death.
Daniel opened the report and went through it. As he absorbed the shocking revelation from the autopsy report, a wave of questions washed over him. He sat back in his office, alone with his thoughts, grappling with the weight of Day's murder and its implications for his own past.

His mind became a whirlwind of memories and suspicions. 'Ricin'; the poison described in the report triggered a flood of recollections from his time as a Soviet py, reminding him of the dangerous world he had once inhabited. In the depths of his rumination, Daniel couldn't help but question the motives behind Day's murder. Was it a calculated act aimed at silencing Day'? If yes, why? Or was it a warning? To who exactly?
A sense of unease settled within him as he considered the possibility that his past

connections were creeping back to him The dark undercurrents of espionage and betrayal threatened to resurface, pulling him back into the treacherous realm he had fought so hard to escape.

That moment Daniel's distrust heightened. He closed his eyes, allowing the weight of his emotions to settle. Mason's involvement would only complicate matters further. Daniel needed to be sure of his next move before revealing his findings. He couldn't afford to make hasty decisions driven by suspicion or mistrust.

In the silence of his office, Daniel thought of a way out. Perhaps hiding this from Mason was not going to be a good move. Mason was his direct superior now; the sooner he could answer these questions, the better.

Daniel's mind was consumed by the revelations he had uncovered. With apprehension and questions, he picked up the phone and dialed Mason's number. After a few rings, Mason's voice came through the receiver.

"Mason, it's Daniel," he began, his tone filled with urgency and SCEPTICISM. "I've discovered something significant regarding Day's death. It seems he was deliberately poisoned.

'Poison. Certainly, he drank himself to death.' Daniel sigh, people like Mason wore an air of competence but are quite oblivious to the world surrounding them.
'It's no ordinary poison. It's a poison used for assassination.'
'Assassination? What sort of poison could that be?'
There was a moment of silence on the other end of the line, and then Mason continued, carrying a hint of concern. "Daniel, if this is true then its troubling

news indeed. The ministry is trying to escape from the demands of the Marxism agitators by letting this lie as low as possible.' Mason sighed like he was exhausted.

'You seem to have a lot on your neck Mason.' Daniel said suspecting Mason had been busy running errands for his superior like a good boy that he is.

'Yes, I was hoping for less controversial news to be honest. I can tell something is off in this case.'

The unexpected agreement from Mason caught Daniel off guard. For a brief moment, his guard lowered as he allowed a tiny flicker of trust to surface. Perhaps his suspicions about Mason had been misguided. It seemed they were both aligned in their pursuit of the truth.

Mason continued, "I think we must address this issue publicly. The national press conference will be held tomorrow. I can reveal a thing or two to the public to show them the developments in Day's case. It will convey that we are actively working to uncover the truth and bring the perpetrators to justice. Nothing too deep like what you've just said. Just to keep the press busy yapping about nothing."

The mention of a press conference startled Daniel. Going public with the information would certainly intensify the investigation and put pressure on those responsible, but it also carried risks. It meant exposing their hand to potential adversaries lurking in the shadows.

Daniel hesitated for a moment, weighing the pros and cons; He also understood that the public scrutiny brought about by the press conference could help shed light on

Day's murder and potentially lead them closer to the truth but he also knew that Mason held a position of power and influence, capable of manipulating the narrative to suit his own agenda. But

Finally, Daniel spoke, his voice laced with caution. "Mason, we must proceed with caution. It all rings sinister to me.'

'What? You're scared of something Daniel could also tell Mason was chuckling.

'Let's ensure we have a solid plan before we go public. I don't want to give our adversaries any advantage."

There was a brief pause on the other end of the line, and Mason replied, his tone more measured. "You're right, Daniel. We need to strategize and ensure that we're one step ahead. I'll gather the necessary resources and arrange a meeting to discuss the details. We'll make sure to expose the truth while protecting ourselves."

Although Daniel's SCEPTICISM hadn't completely vanished, he felt light lift off the pressure on his shoulder. He felt revealed to the extent that other people would be involved in this. The thought of him jamming on his past unexpectedly and all by himself wasn't what he wanted.

Daniel hung up the phone and looked out the window to the busy London Street. The path ahead was still fraught with uncertainty, but the prospect of a public confrontation with the truth was a slight relief. Still, the nagging feeling hovered over him. He could tell he was getting himself into a dangerous game. How and what game was it? He could tell. But there is no going back now for him. Not now.

CHAPTER FIVE

Daniel's blood boiled with anger as he stormed out of the press conference, his frustration reaching its peak. The room was abuzz with journalists scribbling down notes, their cameras capturing every word that Masons spoke. But Daniel knew the truth, and Masons had just twisted it to suit his own narrative just like he thought he would.

The setting of the press conference was grand, held in a historic hall adorned with ornate chandeliers and intricate wall tapestries. The opulence of the surroundings only heightened Daniel's sense of outrage. How could Masons, a man entrusted with upholding justice, manipulate the truth so callously?

Daniel paced back and forth outside the hall, his mind racing with thoughts of betrayal. He clenched his fists, feeling the weight of the deception he had just witnessed. The excellent English air did little to calm his boiling emotions.

"Damn it, Masons!" he muttered under his breath. "You had no right to lie to the press like that. Day's death was not a suicide, and you know it!"

He had known Masons for years and worked alongside him on various cases, but this blatant manipulation of the truth shattered any lingering trust Daniel had in him. Masons were known for cunning, but he had crossed a line this time.

As he walked through the streets of England, the remnants of the press conference still echoing in his mind, Daniel couldn't help but ruminate on Masons' actions. He knew Masons tended to act impulsively, driven by his own self-interest. But this time, it felt personal.

Daniel had invested himself deeply in Day's case. This was beyond Day. This was something more profound and sinister. The Ricin poison and the silent mode of killing. Those were methods used to assassinate spies who went off course.

Daniel had always had this lingering feeling about Day the moment he questioned him on Finnan's death. It was like looking in the mirror to an extent. Still, he wasn't certain. He needed to be sure thing was not some sort of fever or lucid dreaming again. It needed to be reality; he needed to be sure. And if he'll know what to do next.

With each step he took, Daniel's resolve hardened. Mason's deception to the press could only make things a little harder than he thought. He was left alone to wrap his head around all these. To figure things out while standing by the lies his superior had said.

His head swelled with knowing questions. It can't be them pulling the strings behind this charade? They can't be after him again? They certainly are not out to get him back, are they? The puzzle pieces were out of place. Some are perhaps buried in deep dark secrets covered in blood and skeletons. This indeed went far beyond Day's death, Daniel thought. There were forces at play, powerful entities protecting their interests, and Masons was just a pawn in their game.

As Daniel walked through the bustling streets of London, he made a conscious effort to clear his mind of the knowing questions and burnt of anger that had consumed him earlier. He needed to refocus his thoughts and focus on the other crucial details he had uncovered during his investigation. Perhaps paranoia comes with age. 'Brace yourself, old man.' Daniel muttered under his breath.

Lost in thought, Daniel found himself drawn to a nearby park. The serene atmosphere provided a welcome respite from the chaos of the city. As he strolled along the well-manicured pathways, he couldn't help but marvel at the timeless beauty of London's architecture, a testament to its rich history.

The buildings stood tall and proud, their intricate details capturing the essence of the 1957 era. The charm of the old-world craftsmanship enveloped Daniel, momentarily transporting him to a different time. He could almost hear the echoes of footsteps from decades past mingling with the sounds of the present.

The pleasantness of the people he encountered further added to his fascination. He felt a sense of camaraderie, a connection to the spirit of the place. The friendly smiles and polite greetings were as if time had stood still in this corner of the city.

As he continued his leisurely walk, his mind began to wander. The lucid dreams that had plagued him lately once again came to the forefront of his thoughts. These dreams were a bittersweet escape, a glimpse into a world where he could find solace and happiness.

In his dream, Daniel was surrounded by eager students, captivated by his words as he lectured on Charles Dickens. He could see the spark of curiosity in their eyes, their thirst for knowledge mirroring his own. The classroom became a sanctuary where he could share his passion for literature and inspire young minds.

The dream took him to the hallowed halls of a prestigious university, where he roamed the corridors with a sense of purpose. He engaged in intellectual discussions, debating ideas with fellow scholars. The weight of espionage seemed to dissipate in this realm of academia.

But amidst the joy and contentment of the dream, there lingered a tinge of sadness. The stark contrast between this idyllic world and the harsh realities of his present situation was a constant reminder of his choices and the sacrifices he had endured.

As Daniel emerged from his reverie, he couldn't help but feel a pang of longing. His was his temporary escape, a respite from the chaos that consumed his waking hours. It reminded him of the person he could have been, the life he could have led had he not been bamboozled into this.

Yet, he also recognized that dreams, no matter how alluring, were but illusions. The truth awaited him, demanding his attention and unwavering dedication. He couldn't afford to lose himself in the allure of a fantasy world; he had a duty to fulfil and dark truths to uncover.

Daniel continued his walk back through the busy streets of London; as his office was at the corner, his thoughts still lingering on the case at hand, he was momentarily startled by a familiar voice calling out to him. He paused, his attention caught, and turned to see a young lady walking briskly towards him.

"Professor Daniels!" she called out, a mix of excitement and surprise evident in her voice. "Is that really you?"

Daniel recognized the voice before he even saw her face. It was Gilla, his former student from lecturing at St. Petersburg Russian University. The memories flooded back, and a glimmer of a smile tugged at the corner of his lips, though he tried his best to maintain his stoic and uninterested facade.

Gilla closed the distance between them with an enthusiastic stride, her eyes sparkling joyfully. She reached him, slightly out of breath, and extended her hand in greeting. "It's so good to see you! What are you doing here in London?"

Surprised by his excitement on seeing her, Daniel shook her hand, his expression remaining composed. "Gilla, it's been a while. I'm here on business," he replied, his voice steady and professional. "But it's a pleasant surprise to run into you. How have you been?"

Gilla's face lit up as she spoke, her words bubbling enthusiastically. She shared stories of her academic achievements, the progress she had made in her career, and the adventures she had embarked upon since they last met. Her zest for life was infectious, and Daniel found himself slowly thawing, allowing genuine warmth to seep into his demeanour.

They briefly walked down the bustling streets, lost in conversation. Gilla's animated gestures and laughter painted a vibrant backdrop to the ordinary surroundings.

Daniel couldn't help but feel a surge of pride as Gilla recounted her academic successes. She had always been an exceptional student, her thirst for knowledge matched only by her relentless determination. As they reminisced about their time at the university, perhaps it was the reverie he had just enjoyed but that moment, Daniel's stoicism cracked, and he allowed himself to express genuine admiration and delight.

As they wandered through the streets, Gilla's infectious spirit brought a sense of lightness and joy to their shared moments. Her laughter echoed through the air, filling the spaces between their conversations. Despite the passing of time, Gilla's warm personality and unyielding positivity had remained unchanged. She embraced life with an open heart, and her unwavering belief in the power of human connection shone through in every interaction.

Still he couldn't help but notice the subtle changes in Gilla. The young, eager student he once knew had blossomed into a confident and accomplished woman. Her intellectual curiosity remained, but it was now tempered with a wisdom that only experience could bring.

For a brief moment, Daniel allowed himself to fully embrace the joy of the encounter. The weight of the case, the burden of his investigations, momentarily faded into the background. It was a reminder that perhaps Mary was right after all. Life was not solely defined by darkness and deception; there were moments of genuine ephemeral connection and shared humanity that brought solace and rejuvenation.

Gilla, a young lady with short brown hair and sparkling blue eyes, exuded a vibrant, infectious energy. Her vivacious personality and buoyant spirit were evident in every interaction. She had a way of lighting up a room with her presence, her laughter ringing like music.

Her short brown hair framed her face with playfulness, reflecting her willingness to embrace life's adventures. Her eyes, a mesmerizing shade of blue, sparkled with curiosity and intelligence, hinting at the depth of her character.

He had always known Gilla's bubbly personality was the life of any gathering in the university. Her genuine enthusiasm and zest for life drew people to her like moths to a flame. She had a natural gift for making others feel at ease, effortlessly weaving a sense of warmth and camaraderie into her interactions.

One of Gilla's most endearing traits was her quirky sense of humour. She had a knack for finding joy in the simplest things, often surprising her friends and acquaintances with unexpected yet delightful comedic moments. Her wit and clever wordplay brought laughter to even the most mundane situations, leaving a trail of smiles in her wake.

She revelled in playfully teasing her former professor, gently prodding him to let down his guard and show his genuine emotions like she did in her university days. Again, her lighted-hearted mischievous nature broke through Daniel's stoic front, coaxing him into brief moments of amusement and lightheartedness. Their banter created a dynamic that blended respect and camaraderie.

There was an unmistakable air of joy and excitement as she interacted with her former professor, Daniel. Gilla's eyes were happy, and her infectious laughter punctuated their conversations. She looked thrilled to have the opportunity to reconnect with someone who had played a pivotal role in her academic journey.

Gilla's genuine affection and admiration for her professor were palpable. She expressed her gratitude for his guidance and mentorship, acknowledging his impact on her academic and personal growth. Her appreciation was laced with deep respect and a desire to continue learning from his wealth of knowledge.

As Gilla continued to captivate Daniel with her fun and expressive personality, he couldn't help but be reminded of Anna, his ex-wife, during their early years together. Yet, Daniel slowly loses his surprise that he finds himself absorbed in the presence of just gee and light-heartedness. The parallels between Gilla's infectious energy and Anna's vibrant spirit stirred bittersweet memories within him.

Daniel and Anna had been like two sides of a coin, complete opposites in many ways. Where he was reserved and analytical, Anna was outgoing and spontaneous. Their differences, however, had initially drawn them together, as they complemented each other in ways that seemed to defy logic.

Initially, their love had been an exhilarating whirlwind, their shared moments filled with laughter, adventure, and a profound sense of connection. Their lives intertwined seamlessly, and the world felt vibrant and alive. Daniel reminisced about the happy times they had spent together, the shared dreams and aspirations that had once seemed unbreakable.

But as the years passed, the cracks in their relationship began to surface. The same qualities that had drawn them together became sources of friction. Their differences, once charming, now seemed irreconcilable. Their paths began to diverge, and the spark once ignited their love faded.

The dissolution of their marriage had been painful and heart-wrenching for both Daniel and Anna. Something he had never admitted to himself till now. The memories of their divorce were like an open wound that never fully healed. The hurt and disappointment lingered, casting a shadow over the sweetness of their early years together.

Daniel couldn't help but feel a pang of sadness as he watched Gilla's vibrant presence. She reminded him of a time when he had felt truly alive when love had illuminated his world. But the memory of that happiness was tainted by the subsequent heartbreak and the lingering bitterness of their failed marriage.

Gilla's resemblance to Anna served as a poignant reminder of love's complexity and relationships' fragility. A complexity he wasn't ready or interested in putting up with again.

Though he found solace in the moments shared with Gilla, her presence provided a temporary respite from the weight of his past. But beneath the surface, he hated returning to moments of vulnerability and openness. He hated the light-hearted feeling he felt, the feeling of pride and the feeling of joy.

As they continued their walk through the bustling streets of London, Daniel's mind became consumed with the memories of his past and the uncertainties of his future. The relief he felt in Gilla's presence became tinged with trepidation. The mere idea of light-heartedness and excitement filled him with a sense of anguish, overshadowing the happiness he found in Gilla's company. Therefore, Daniel remained guarded, his emotions shielded behind a stoic facade.

As they reached the end of their walk, Daniel and Gilla, Daniel briefly nodded at Gilla, bidding her farewell and walked on. Gilla yelled her farewell to him as he worked, promising to stay in touch. Daniel left behind a trail of warmth and inspiration and disappeared into the cold busy street. This was the first time Daniel had thought of Anna in years, and though the thought started with a hone-sweet feeling of warmth and softness. It left a bitter, sour sting taste in his mouth later.

CHAPTER SIX

Daniel entered his office the next day, thinking about the next step to take in the case. Mary approached him quickly with news that the office had assigned an assistant to him. That was strange. He never asked for one as after the mess up of the conference with Mason he was not sure he needed one. ‘What do you mean assistant? He asked Mary. ‘Well you are always constantly complaining that you were getting old at the brink of retirement....’ ‘I don't do that...’ Daniel stopped, surprised that his thoughts had morphed into words all these days. ‘Yes you do...look, there you go’ Mary said excited for him. She had always hoped and pray he found good use of company and now the answer had finally came.

He took the file and was taken aback to discover that Gilla, the vibrant young lady from the streets of London, was not just also part of the investigative force but she was the one assigned to assist him. The realization that Gilla would be assigned to assist him with the case hit him like a wave of conflicting emotions.

When they had first met, Gilla had mentioned her involvement in the force, but it had seemed distant and inconsequential at the time. Now, confronted with the reality that she would be directly involved in his investigation, Daniel felt a mix of surprise, frustration, and resistance.

He couldn't shake off the feeling that Gilla's presence reflected his perceived weakness. He had spent a lifetime cultivating independence and self-reliance, and the thought of relying on someone else, especially someone he had just reconnected with, didn't sit well with him. The idea that others saw him as a middle-aged man needing assistance left a bitter taste in his mouth.

Daniel's initial reaction was one of immediate rejection. He threw the paper away and stormed to Mason's office. He felt a surge of pride, a determination to prove that he was still capable of handling the case independently. He believed that his years of experience and expertise were enough to navigate the complexities of the investigation without any assistance, especially from someone who, in his mind, represented his own vulnerabilities.

He met Gilla on his way to Mason's office and approached her, his tone laced with an air of resistance and his face held a firm frown. "I appreciate the offer, but I prefer to work alone. I have my methods, and I don't need anyone else to intervene," he stated, his voice firm and resolute.

'Profess...sorry Inspector Daniel. I have to say, I'm quite as surprised as you are. You didn't even mention you were here.' Gilla said with a surprised look on her face. But Daniel's frown remained. Undeterred by Daniel reaction, met his resistance with a compassionate understanding. 'I think this will be good for us both. You get the help you require to continue the investigation, while I learn from your brilliant expertise and methods.'

She acknowledged his pride and the desire to prove himself, but gently reminded him that they were part of a team, each with unique skills and perspectives to contribute. "Daniel, I understand your hesitation, but the truth is, we all need support at times," Gilla said with sincerity. "Working together doesn't diminish your abilities or accomplishments."

Reluctantly, Daniel began to reconsider his stance. He couldn't ignore that Gilla's intelligence and keen instincts had impressed him during their brief encounter. She had demonstrated a sharpness that he couldn't overlook, and deep down, he knew that her assistance could potentially make a difference in helping him sort things out.

Still, anyone but Gilla. What happened to the young male competent officers in the office. He wasn't about to put up with Gilla's gee and light-heartedness.

Gilla continued with a spark of determination gleaming in her eyes. 'I respect your experience and leadership.

This could just speed things up a little." Gilla's voice sounded like a broken radio to Daniel. The thought of her trying to speed things up made him even more irritated. Speed things up and cover all evidences with it. At this point it seems that's what Mason is trying to accomplish. Daniel stormed off leaving for his office.

During the day, Daniel heard that Graham wants to see him and was expecting reports on the investigation. As Daniel prepared to give his report on the case, he felt disgust and annoyance from his earlier interaction. He knew his findings would be pivotal in shedding light on the truth behind Day's death. However, he couldn't ignore the tension in the air due to his rift with Mason.

Walking into the chief constable's office, Daniel noticed the stern expression on Graham's face. It was no longer tea time and small talk. The atmosphere was charged with a sense of seriousness, underscoring the importance of the meeting. Mason stood nearby, his demeanor reflecting a mixture of discomfort and apprehension.

Graham motioned for Daniel to take a seat, his gaze unwavering. "Daniel, I've heard about the disagreements between you and Mason regarding handling this case. I must say, I'm disappointed in Mason's unprofessional behaviour," Graham stated firmly, turning to Mason. 'I've spoken to him about this and there will be another press conference to clear the air on the irregularities of the case.' Mason nodded, looking down in accepted defeat.

That took Daniel by surprise. But he felt a mixture of relief and validation hearing Graham's words. It reassured him that his concerns about Mason's conduct were justified and that his perspective was being acknowledged. "Like discussed with Mason. I suspect foul play. Day didn't kill himself. Ricin is not easily accessible here in England. He could have gone for other common poison here, but not one from people he claims to be a part of.'

As he spoke, he saw the concern on Graham's face and the surprise that flickered in Mason's eyes. Graham listened intently, his expression shifting from stern to thoughtful. After Daniel finished his report, a moment of silence hung in the room as the gravity of the situation settled in. Finally, Graham broke the silence.

"Daniel, I appreciate your diligence and thoroughness in uncovering the truth. Your findings are troubling, to say the least," Graham responded and sighed deeply, his voice reflecting concern and determination. "It is clear that we need to pursue this investigation further, and I have no doubt that you are the right person for the job." he said finally

Turning his attention to Mason,. "We are still sticking to the plan Mason," he said knowingly. 'Still, I must express my disappointment in your conduct. It is unacceptable for an officer of your position to rush to conclusions without concrete evidence. This kind of behaviour undermines the integrity of our department."

Mason visibly shifted under Graham's reproach, his gaze falling to the ground. "I...I apologize...'

Daniel couldn't help but feel a sense of vindication hearing Graham reprimand Mason. At least someone was there to put him under check.

Graham then turned his attention back to Daniel, his voice filled with confidence. "Daniel, you were placed in charge of this investigation for a reason. I trust your abilities and your commitment to uncovering the truth. Use all the resources available, and keep me informed of any significant developments."

'Thanks Graham' still Daniel knew he could push the case of his new unwanted assistant under the rug.

'About the young happy woman...' Daniel started. As Daniel expressed his reservations about Gilla assisting him with the case, Graham listened attentively, his expression thoughtful. When Daniel finished voicing his concerns, Graham sighed and leaned back in his chair, and shook his head in disapproval

"Daniel, I understand your hesitation in working with Gilla," Graham began, his tone measured. "But I have to disagree with you on this matter. Gilla has proven herself to be an intelligent and capable officer. Her insights and perspectives may provide a fresh approach to the investigation."

Daniel's brows furrowed, his SCEPTICISM still lingering. "Graham, you know me long enough to know how much I love solitude. I've always worked alone, and I've been successful in my past cases. I fear that involving someone unfamiliar with my methods might hinder progress."

Graham nodded, acknowledging Daniel's point of view. "I appreciate your track record and preference for working independently, Daniel. But, we need to adapt and embrace new perspectives. Gilla brings her own strengths to the table, and by working together, you both have the potential to achieve better results."

Why was everyone saying the same thing Daniel thought wearily?

‘I believe that with your leadership and Gilla's abilities, you two can make significant progress in this case."

***

Daniel resumed his duties at the office, his mind still grappling with the weight of recent revelations. Since he can’t successfully get rid of Gilla. He tolerated her, keeping to himself and not involving her in too much of his findings. He mostly sends her on simple errands to get rid of her when he doesn't want her around. But most times the errands were done excellently well and had proven useful to further the investigation.

Regardless of how pleased he was Daniel made a conscious effort to ensure he doesn't get too fond of her.

As they delved deeper into the investigation, Daniel couldn't shake the memory of his last interview with Day at the espresso bar. He was sent by the department to do more findings on those associated with Finnan after his suicide. They needed to be sure he didn't have more recruits in the university. It was a pivotal moment to ascertain Day's innocence and distance him from any involvement with the Soviet Union. Now that Daniel thought about it, he wasn't certain he had heard if he heard the things he wanted to hear from Day, or if he had heard the right things.

Sipping their espresso, the aroma of freshly brewed coffee filled the air as Daniel and Day engaged in that conversation. Day shared stories of his academic pursuits, intellectual curiosity, and passion for social justice. The more they spoke, the clearer it became that Day's intentions were rooted in a genuine desire for a better world, untainted by the murky politics of espionage that the ministry had thought he was involved in.

In that moment, Daniel had seen a flicker of light in Day’s eye when Day gave him a knowing look and he returned it. It was nothing at that moment but now it's everything. Was he aware of who he was? Were they both playing the same game but had no idea they were players? Daniel was quite determined to ensure Day was proven to have nothing to do with the traitor Finnan.

Now, with Gilla by his side, Daniel sought to ensure she uncover any overlooked clues that might shed light on Day's death.

Together, they meticulously combed through the evidence, poring over documents, testimonies, and anything that could offer a glimmer of insight into the truth.

While Daniel's mind, like a puzzle with missing pieces, tirelessly worked to fill in the gaps. He found solace in the moments of quiet reflection, his thoughts drifting back to the espresso bar, where he and Day had shared a fleeting moment of respite amidst a world filled with uncertainty. It was a memory he held onto tightly, it was probably the only clue that really mattered to digging things out.

But with each step forward, Daniel couldn't shake the nagging feeling of trepidation. Finnan’s case had shook the ministry hard; there were fears that his ties could go deep implicating individuals within the British police and military. The implications were staggering, hinting at a web of espionage and betrayal that threatened to plunge the nation into chaos. But no one had any clear proof and he suspected no one wanted too because they were either involved or were scared to be involved.

As the weight of their findings pressed upon him, Daniel's determination wavered. Doubt crept into his mind, fueled by the vastness of the conspiracy they were unearthing. Gilla had traced the Ricin poison that killed Day directly to the Soviet Union. He was clearly assassinated. But why? He wondered if their pursuit of the truth would lead to justice or if it would merely scratch the surface of a much larger, more insidious plot. The latter which he hopes he doesn't get involved in.

Still, as he sat in his office, surrounded by stacks of files and evidence, Daniel felt a flicker of hope ignite within him. The weight of the investigation bore down on his shoulders, but he refused to let it crush his spirit. He hates to admit it but Gilla's unwavering support became a lifeline for Daniel. Her sharp intellect and unwavering dedication to the case provided him with a glimmer of hope amidst the darkness that threatened to consume him.

Mary was amazing with the job, but she was not as sophisticated as Gilla was in. Gilla meticulously analyzed every piece of information they had gathered, cross-referenced testimonies, examined surveillance footage, and dug deeper into the lives of those implicated in the assassination. Still every lead he pursued brought her closer to the heart of the darkness, but also revealed the immense complexity of the situation he found themselves in.

As the pieces of the puzzle fell into place, Daniel's determination only grew stronger. He couldn't turn a blind eye to the darkness lurking in the shadows, threatening not just him, but the very fabric of the society he had come to love.

In moments of solitude, Daniel found himself reflecting on the essence of justice. He grappled with the moral complexities of his role as an investigator, questioning whether the pursuit of truth justified the toll it exacted. But deep within his heart, he knew that the answers they sought held the power to bring about change and protect the innocent from future harm.

As he closed his eyes for a brief moment of respite, Daniel drew a deep breath. The storm was approaching, he knew, and he was ready to face it head-on.

In that moment, the realization hit Daniel like a thunderbolt, causing his heart to skip a beat. The deaths of Finnan and Day, both by suicide and occurring within such proximity, could not be mere coincidence. There had to be a deeper connection, a hidden truth that eluded him until now.

He furrowed his brow, his mind racing as he retraced their steps, trying to uncover any missed clues or overlooked details. How had he not seen the pattern before? Finnan, the once vibrant police officer turned suspected Soviet spy, and Day, the enigmatic figure with ties to both Finnan and ideology of the Soviet Union. Their deaths were not isolated incidents.

Daniel couldn't dismiss the thought that there was a sinister force at play, orchestrating these tragedies for their own twisted purposes. It was no longer just an investigation into the death of one individual but two individuals who could have close links to the damning shadows that hunt him in the dark.

He leaned back in his chair, his mind racing through the possibilities. Could it be really true that Finnan and Day were more than just acquaintances? Did they share a common purpose or a secret that had pushed them to take such drastic measures? The weight of these questions bore down on him, demanding answers that seemed to elude him at every turn.

'Get me the files on Finnan's death. I intend to know how he killed himself.'

'Okay sir,' Gilla said and quickly stepped out. She returned soon with a file. 'I was told this was highly confidential and it must be returned as soon as possible.' Gilla said as Daniel snatched the file off her hands.

He scanned through them as soon as he could till he arrived at the autopsy report section. Finnan too had died from the poison Ricin. Daniel tightened his gaze on the report to be sure he was seeing the right thing. Was Ricin now common in England or was this another assassination? Daniel thought.

'Are you okay?' Gilla's voice brought him back to the present moment, jolting him out of his deep contemplation. 'You've been quiet for a minute now.' She looked at him, with a searching look, like she wanted to be sure of the things that were currently going on in his mind.

He waved Gilla's concerns off. But the air in his office felt heavy, suffused with an unsettling mix of intrigue and apprehension. He mulled over the evidence he had gathered, retracing his steps through the investigation, searching for any missed clues or overlooked details.

His mind raced with possibilities and theories, each one more perplexing than the last. Were Finnan and Day somehow entangled in a web of espionage? Did their paths intersect through a shared connection to the Soviet Union? Or was there something deeper, something more sinister lurking beneath the surface?

Daniel's instincts told him that there was more to Day's deaths than met the eye and he was right. Now he was sure his instinct was telling him the same thing with these two. He couldn't shake the feeling that they were pawns in a much larger game, caught in a web of secrets and betrayals. It gnawed at him, the nagging sensation that the truth lay just beyond his grasp, waiting to be unraveled.

Frustration mounted within Daniel, his desire for answers growing more urgent with each passing minute. He knew he couldn't ignore the significance of the shared fate between Finnan and Day. Their suicides were more than random occurrences; they held the key to a deeper truth, truths blended into the shadows of the night.

He knew that the darkness that lurked behind the veil of secrets was vast and unforgiving. It whispered of danger and peril, warning him of the consequences that awaited those who dared to venture too far. For he knew that the connection between their deaths held the key to a truth that had the power to shake the very foundations of the world he had come to love.

In that moment of clarity, Daniel felt a surge of adrenaline burst of anger through his veins. He got up and walked to Mason's office. Daniel entered Mason's office with a determined stride, his gaze unwavering. The weight of the investigation and the burden of the truth bore down on him, fueling his resolve to confront the man before him. Mason, knew about the Ricin poison and the closely approximate suicide of Finnan and Day. But Finnan's case had been swept under the rug deliberately.

As he met Mason's gaze, Daniel felt a mix of anger and frustration simmering within him. The department had uncovered the damning evidence connecting Finnan to the Soviet Union, a revelation sent shockwaves through the department, and his suicide was highly suspicious. Yet, it had been brushed aside.

"Why, Mason?" Daniel's voice was laced with accusation. "Why was Finnan's case not given the same attention as Day's?

Why wasn't the issue of their both use of Ricin for their suicide raised?"

Mason leaned back in his chair, his face bearing the weariness of a man caught in the intricate web of politics. He sighed, his gaze shifting momentarily before meeting Daniel's eyes again. "Daniel, it's a complicated situation. You have a case on Day, just focus on that'

'How can I focus on Day he was intertwined with Finnan? The last time I checked Finnan's case was closed on suicide.'

Mason ran his hands through his brows to his temples massaging it slightly. 'You better than anyone else should have understood the delicate nature of this situation. Aren't you the sharpest mind in the office? Finnan found out about his ties to the Soviet Union as a police officer. If that was made public, would not only tarnish his and our reputations, but also cast doubt on the entire police force and military."

Daniel clenched his fists, his frustration mounting. It was not just about Finnan and Day's likely dual involvement in Soviet Union espionage. It was more of his past writing a letter of invitation back to the darkness. He was the fact that he too could soon become involved in the betrayal within the ranks.

"Don't you think there's a danger here we need to uncover? We talked about Day's case been deeper than what it looks the last time and it turned out true'

Mason's expression hardened, his voice tinged with resignation. "We live in a world where politics and national security dictate our actions Daniel. The repercussions of exposing Finnan's true allegiance has far-reaching consequences. We must tread carefully."

Daniel's eyes burned with a mix of anger and irritation. Why was Mason talking like a politician to his electorate? "Tread carefully? By keeping this hidden, are we not perpetuating a system of corruption and manipulation?' It was important to Daniel that everything comes to the light of the public. Maybe some pressure could tighten the restriction of any further infiltration of Soviet espionage into England that could come for him.

Mason sighed heavily, his gaze softening with a hint of understanding. "You've got a point, sure you do. But sometimes, the greater good requires difficult choices. Exposing Finnan's ties to the Soviet Union could spark public unrest. It could compromise ongoing operations, and put lives at risk. Can we at least strike a balance between justice and protecting the integrity of our institutions?"

Daniel's resolve hardened, his voice firm. "Mason, there must be a way. We can't let fear of the consequences silence the truth." he hoped Mason didn't see through this act. He was carving out ways to protect himself using the knowledge of the tragedy of others. Daniel held his breath and held himself back from saying anything else. He realized he was truly afraid for the first time in a long time.

'I find it strange that you're acting naive Daniel. You know that even if Day and finnan were caught up in the same web of deception they cannot be treated as two equal people with equal punishment. Day was a public Marxist. He earned the admiration of the university and his friends, converting some of them. Some still take to the streets today to protest and demand Marxism.'

"So, you're saying that in Day's case, a university student runs deeper than Finnan who was an officer of the law and likely has close ties with ranks in the police and military?'

'I'm saying Day is given more attention because of the potential political repercussions his involvement with Marxism could have?" Mason snapped. 'Day's connection to Marxism, particularly his influence in university circles, raised concerns among higher authorities. There was a fear that his actions could ignite a broader movement, leading to political unrest and potentially even a revolution. We can't afford to underestimate the power of ideological fervor, especially among the younger generation."

Daniel's mind raced as he contemplated the implications of Mason's words. It was a delicate balancing act, balancing justice and preserving social stability. Two weight rested on his shoulder now; the weight of the responsibility pressed heavily on his shoulders, knowing that any misstep could have far-reaching consequences and the weight of self-preservation against the likelihood of the shadows showing up to him

‘We must find a way to balance the scales of justice without plunging our society into chaos. It's a difficult path to tread, but c’mon Dan, let's face reality!"

Daniel's mind churned, grappling with the ethical and moral dilemmas that lay before him. He remained quiet carefully with his lips now so he would mutter any more desperate word.

'Day is fuckin Jewish!' Mason continued. 'We don't want to be accused of starting another holocaust do we?' Mason took a deep breath to calm his nerves. 'The wounds inflicted by the Holocaust are still fresh in our society's collective memory. We can't risk sending the wrong message or fueling the prevailing prejudices.'

"I understand the responsibility we bear," Daniel finally said. His eyes rested on the floor, not in shame but in weariness. This case was already eating right through his skin into his bones. It was complex, irritating and weighted heavily on his shoulders like a big wet foam.

As the day wore on, Daniel could feel the weariness seeping into his bones. The weight of the investigation, the complexities of the cases, and the historical implications weighed heavily on his mind. He knew he needed a respite, a moment of solace to recharge his spirit.

Leaving the precinct behind, Daniel made his way home. The evening air felt crisp against his face, offering a gentle reprieve from the demands of the day. Unlocking the door, he stepped into the comforting embrace of his humble abode.

With a sigh of relief, Daniel shed the weight of his professional responsibilities. He kicked off his shoes, allowing the coolness of the wooden floor to soothe his tired feet. The familiar scent of home embraced him, wrapping him in a sense of familiarity and sanctuary.

In the living room, the soft glow of the lamp beckoned him. The shelves lined with books whispered promises of escapism, knowledge, and adventure. But tonight, Daniel sought a different kind of solace. He craved the cathartic release that only the flickering screen could offer.

Settling into his favorite armchair, Daniel reached for the remote control and powered on the television. The familiar opening credits of Casablanca began to play, their soothing melody a balm to his weary soul. It was a film he had watched countless times before, yet each viewing offered a comforting familiarity.

As the story unfolded on the screen, Daniel lost himself in the narrative. The characters became his companions, their struggles and triumphs his own. For a brief moment, he could set aside the complexities of his own life and immerse himself in the lives of others.

A bottle of beer stood on the side table, its chilled glass perspiring in the warmth of the room. Daniel reached for it, relishing in the satisfying pop of the cap being released. The amber liquid poured into the waiting glass, its effervescence dancing with anticipation.

Sipping the beer, Daniel savored its bitter notes, allowing the flavors to cascade over his palate. The coolness trickled down his throat, momentarily washing away the fatigue and worry that had plagued him throughout the day. He closed his eyes, letting the momentary bliss wash over him.

As the movie played on, Daniel's mind drifted, his thoughts wandering to the events of the day. He replayed the conversations, the revelations, and the complexities that had unfolded before him. It was impossible to completely set aside the weight of the investigation, but in this quiet respite, he could momentarily suspend the burden.

Lost in his thoughts, Daniel reached for the remote control and switched to the evening news. The world outside his sanctuary filtered in, reminding him of the vastness of the challenges beyond his own investigation. News anchors discussed political upheavals of the Marxist agitators. He quickly switched back to the movie.

With each passing moment, Daniel felt the weight of the day's exhaustion slowly dissipating. The combination of the movie, the beer, and the news provided a catharsis—an opportunity to decompress, to reflect, and to find solace in the simplicity of these familiar rituals.

As the night wore on, Daniel allowed himself to be fully present in the moment. Rick and Lisa said their final goodbyes and Lisa took off to America. Daniel was left with a feeling of satisfaction after this.

With a contented sigh and an empty beer bottle, Daniel switched off the television, and the room got enveloped by a gentle darkness. As the room fell into darkness, Daniel found himself drifting into a sea of memories. The flickering images of the movie were replaced by the vivid recollection of his past, and in that moment, his thoughts turned to Anna.

It had been years since their paths diverged, since their once-unbreakable bond had shattered. They had been two souls intertwined in a fiery dance of love and passion, yet as time wore on, their differences began to overshadow their shared desires. They had become strangers within the confines of their own relationship.

But as the solitude of the evening settled around him, Daniel couldn't help but feel a pang of longing, a deep ache that resonated from the depths of his being. He missed the way Anna's laughter would fill the room, the way her eyes would sparkle with mischief. He missed the way her touch could ignite a fire within him, erasing all worries and doubts.

The memories flooded back with an intensity that caught him off guard. He remembered the early days of their friendship, when they were both young and full of dreams. She had been drawn to each him like iron on magnet while Daniel was busy avoiding bullets and making his mark in his profession. He soon found himself drawn first to her passion for him and then to her. They were two totally different people but their differences only served as a magnetism that fueled their connection.

Anna had possessed an allure, an unconventional beauty that had captivated him from the start. Her long blonde hair framed a face that exuded both strength and vulnerability. Her eyes, a piercing shade of blue, held a depth that hinted at a world of emotions waiting to be discovered. She had a way of commanding attention, effortlessly drawing people into her orbit and her air excluded sophistication and class.

Their love had been a whirlwind, a tempestuous affair that transcended logic and reason. They were opposites in so many ways—Anna's free-spirited nature clashed with Daniel's analytical mind—Her expensive classy taste clashed with his lack of self-consciousness in his looks.

Daniel recalled a time when he and Anna had discussed having children. They were seated on their cozy couch in their living room, engaged in a lighthearted conversation about their future. The topic of having children had somehow made its way into their discussion, sparking both curiosity and laughter.

Daniel, with a wide grin on his face, expressed his excitement about the prospect of starting a family. He painted vivid pictures of playing catch in the park, teaching little ones how to ride a bicycle, and the joy of witnessing their first steps.

Anna, on the other hand, had a mischievous twinkle in her eyes as she playfully countered Daniel's enthusiasm. While she adored children, the thought of sleepless nights, dirty diapers, and endless responsibilities made her a bit apprehensive. She preferred the idea of freedom and spontaneity, unburdened by the demands of parenthood.

Their conversation took a comical turn as they delved into the quirks and challenges of raising children. Daniel couldn't help but share stories from his childhood about the trials and tribulations of parenting. He recounted tales of temper tantrums in the supermarket, messy food fights at the dinner table, and the comical mishaps that seemed to accompany every milestone.

Anna listened intently, her laughter filling the room as she imagined the chaos that parenthood often entailed. She playfully teased Daniel about his eagerness, jokingly suggesting that he should experience taking care of a mischievous toddler for a week before committing to the idea.

In that moment, as Daniel recalled their amusing conversation, he couldn't help but feel a sense of irritation. Was he that dumb? How could he have children when he was actively involved in espionage then? He was glad he recognized the truth in Anna's words, and listened to her. He had no idea what he was into but he was glad she stopped him from that decision

As the memories of that conversation filled his mind, Daniel couldn't help but chuckle to himself. He appreciated the humor in the realization that decision, once viewed with uncertainty, had ultimately reduced the chaos in his life to a bare minimum.

It was sad that what had been what precisely initially ignited their passion became a major focus in tearing it down.

As the years passed, their once-flaming love had gradually dimmed. The weight of their divergent paths, the pressures of their individual aspirations, and the unspoken compromises had taken their toll. Their once-shared dreams had become distant echoes, overshadowed by the complexities of life.

Daniel thought of the moments that led to their eventual separation—the arguments, the unspoken resentments, the moments of silent retreat. They had both been wounded, scarred by the realization that their love could no longer bridge the vast expanse that had grown between them.

Yet, despite the pain of their separation, Daniel couldn't help but yearn for what once was. He missed the comfort of Anna's presence, the way she could understand him without the need for words. He missed the way their lives had intertwined, the shared moments of laughter and tears.

But as the longing washed over him, Daniel also felt a tinge of regret. He wondered if perhaps he had not cared hard enough. If he had allowed his ego to overshadow the love that had once burned so fiercely.

In the depths of the night, Daniel allowed himself to succumb to the waves of nostalgia, the bittersweet embrace of memories. He closed his eyes and the sound of Anna's laughter echoed in his ears, reminding him of the joy they had found in their path. He acknowledged the pain of his longing, the unfulfilled desires that lingered within him. But he also recognized the need to move forward, to let go of what could no longer be.

With a deep breath, Daniel resolved to focus on the present, on the investigation at hand. Dwelling on the past made him feel weakened, it was no use, he thought. Anna belonged to a different chapter of his life—a chapter that had been shut long ago.

CHAPTER SEVEN

Finnan had been in the force way earlier than Daniel. Finnan was a young and vibrant police officer who joined the force with a strong sense of justice and a desire to make a difference. He was intelligent, diligent, and highly regarded by his colleagues, including Daniel, who had taken Finnan under his wing.

From the outside, Finnan was the epitome of loyalty and dedication to his job. He was known for his impeccable work ethic and unwavering commitment to upholding the law. However, beneath the surface, his deep secret moves were concealed.

No one could ever suspect Finnan had long been a recruited spy who was recruited by the Soviet Union. He had been carefully selected and groomed, trained to blend seamlessly into the police force and gather valuable intelligence for his handlers. Finnan's double life was a carefully constructed facade, and he played his part skillfully, earning the trust and respect of his colleagues.

Suspicions first began when confidential information from the British intelligence community started leaking out and several pieces of information were compromised because of this. There were several suspects, but no exact perpetrator. Finnan had also started befriending several officers in the rank, including high ranking ones and officers in the military. No one could swear it was him.

A counterintelligence operation was soon launched. Daniel was chosen to conduct an anonymous interview on Finnan and many others on the possibilities of being involved in the compromising action that could spell them out as spies. This is because the clues and anomalies hinted at a mole within the police force, but the identity of the spy remained elusive. Yet, pressure to uncover the traitor mounted, and suspicions eventually fell on Finnan.

One fateful day, an operation led by British authorities exposed Finnan's true allegiance, Finnan was known to love pretty women, he had a beautiful wife himself. So he was set up by a tall blonde-haired police officer who offered her to be recruited into his web of espionage. Finnan hesitated at first, unsuspecting of the trap set for him. But with the constant pressing of the pretty female officer, he found good use to her and opened up on his agreements with the Soviets. She got all the evidence against him to the force in files and documents, which till these day was sealed as inaccessible and confidential by the department.

The shocking revelation sent shockwaves through the entire police department. Officers who had once seen him as a trusted comrade now viewed him with a mix of anger, betrayal, and disbelief. Finnan's arrest and subsequent interrogation were swift and intense. He was confronted with the evidence of his espionage, and he had no choice but to admit to his double life.

The fallout from Finnan's exposure was significant. The authorities moved swiftly to sever all ties with him, stripping him of his badge and dismissing him from the force. The colleagues who had once admired him now turned their backs, unable to reconcile the image of the dedicated officer with the reality of the spy in their midst.

The impact of his actions reverberated throughout the force, everyone was a suspect. And to heighten everyone's suspicion the female officer that helped prove Finnan's guilt was quickly transferred and soon became no were to be found. Rumors spread around the office that the files she found out implicated some police officers who were already in the force and it could send more shockwaves through the nation. So Finnan's case was buried under the rocks. While officers got copied with a new case to keep their minds away from Finnan.

Daniel, who had been one of Finnan's closest allies, felt a profound sense of betrayal. Considering Finnan's action rang a big hefty bell of his past life. This is was the beginning of the end for Daniel. Yet, he put on a bravado front and did what was needful by disassociating himself from Finnan so he wouldn't be counted a suspect. He had barely escaped several attempts in the past to be found out and now that he was out, he doesn't intend to get linked with what he had done away with.

For Daniel, the experience left an indelible mark on his career and personal life. He was haunted by the realization that he had failed to see the truth about Finnan, questioning his own ability to discern loyalty from deceit. A thought had crossed him that perhaps this was a payback for his years in espionage too. However, he refused to admit to any damning effect his actions could have caused on anyone and brushed off the thought as irrelevant.

In the aftermath of Finnan's exposure, the department implemented new, stricter protocols and measures to prevent such infiltration in the future. However, the scars of Finnan's betrayal was one that echoes through the walls of the precinct. It rang through the shadows like a damning bell like a precursor to more deep secret revelations.

That same night of that day, Daniel made his way to the theatre to see Finnan's wife, Amelia, perform on stage. The night was cold and crisp as he stepped in. He had known her for several years, having been introduced to her by Finnan himself. Amelia was a popular actress in the theatre. She had an unconventional beauty and possessed a charming sex appeal that seemed to captivate the audience whenever she graced the stage.

As Daniel entered the theatre, the air was filled with anticipation. The dimly lit auditorium buzzed with whispers and the rustling of programs. He found his seat and settled in, his gaze fixed on the stage, but his mind wandered off to Finnan's case. Wondering what could become of him next. British intelligence was surely coming for him. It was only a matter of minutes before he was no longer a free man. It was only a matter of minutes before Amelia realized she may no longer have a husband.

The curtains slowly rose, revealing a meticulously crafted set, transporting the audience to a bygone era. The stage came alive with a burst of energy as the actors immersed themselves in their roles. And then, amidst the collective hush, Amelia made her grand entrance.

She commanded the stage with an effortless grace, drawing every eye towards her. Her presence was magnetic, a potent combination of confidence and vulnerability. With each movement, she exuded a raw and captivating energy that was impossible to ignore.

Amelia's voice, like velvet, filled the theatre as she delivered her lines with precision and emotion. Her expressive eyes conveyed a depth of feeling that touched the hearts of those in the audience, including Daniel's.

As the play unfolded, Daniel tried to connect with the story displayed right in front of him, but his attention solely focused on Amelia. Her every gesture, every inflection in her voice, held a profound significance. He wondered if she too was involved with Finnan. Since finnan wanted more recruited as the days, perhaps he had looked into the potential of his popular actress wife delivering seasoned information to his informants

Amelia's performance was a tapestry of emotions, ranging from moments of vulnerability and tenderness to fiery passion and resolute determination. She effortlessly weaved through the complexities of her character, leaving a lasting impression on all who witnessed her artistry.

In the midst of the applause that erupted at the end of the play, Daniel felt a mix of emotions wash over him. Admiration for Amelia's talent, yes, but also a deep sense of longing and regret. He couldn't help but reflect on his connection with Finnan, was Finnan also aware he had been involved earlier? Was he been monitored by the shadows he had left behind who as he just realized had been lurking close to him all these while.

After the performance, Daniel made his way to the exit, walking through the deserted streets of the city. The night air was still, and the city lights cast a soft glow upon the pavement. His mind replayed Amelia's performance, the beauty and vulnerability she had conveyed with such artistry.

In that moment, Daniel longed for a simpler existence, one free from the shadows of deceit and uncertainty. He yearned for a life where he could revel in the beauty of art and talent without the weight of his past haunting him. But as much as he wished for it, he knew that his reality was far from that ideal.

The night wrapped around him like a cloak, muffling the sounds of the city and casting a veil of solitude upon his thoughts. He walked aim to get a Taxi soon, as his mind involuntarily sunk into a sea of memories and regrets.

The echoes of laughter and shared adventures resonated in his mind, a stark contrast to the silence that now surrounded him. It was in those moments, and probably the only time that he felt the weight of the choices he had made. The life of a spy had always been a double-edged sword, a dance between loyalty and betrayal. In his quest for information and power, he had sacrificed friendships and trust, leaving a trail of broken connections in his wake. He, unlike Finnan, was lucky enough not to be found out.

Amelia's performance had momentarily transported him back to a time when life was simpler, when he lived only for the good pleasures of life like wine, literature, women and money. His purpose was clear, and his path seemed straight. But the harsh reality of his past choices lingered, reminding him that he could never fully escape the consequences of his actions.

The night pressed on, and Daniel found himself at the edge of the city, staring out into the vast expanse of darkness. The stars twinkled above, distant and unattainable, mirroring the dreams and aspirations he once held dear. But now, those dreams felt like distant echoes, faded and elusive.

As the night wore on, Daniel felt a sense of resignation settle within him. He accepted that he couldn't change the past or rewrite the choices he had made. The only path forward was to confront the truth, to navigate the murky waters of his present reality, and to find a semblance of redemption amidst the shadows.

He soon made his way back to his apartment, as he unlocked the door and stepped inside, he couldn't shake off the unease that had settled within him.

It was then that his phone rang, piercing the silence of the room. With a sense of foreboding, he picked up the receiver and heard the voice of Mary on the other end. Her words were measured and heavy with sorrow as she delivered the news that would shake Daniel to his core.

"Finnan... he's gone, Daniel," Mary uttered, her voice trembling with disbelief. "They found him dead already this morning. He killed himself!"

A chill ran down Daniel's spine as the weight of the news settled upon him. He cleared his throat quietly and offered some words to calm Mary down. As much as he knew this was inevitable for Finan he couldn't shake off the shock he felt that moment. He recalled his last talk with Finnan, he had delivered the news that he was cleared of any charges the department could place on him and he was free to go. Even though they both knew he wasn't really going to be free any time soon.

As the news of Finnan's suicide spread, the shock reverberated through the department. But instead of mourning the loss of a dedicated officer, the whispers and hushed conversations revolved around speculation and rumors. The department was not interested in uncovering any truth behind Finnan's tragic end. And his case was closed on suicide.

Seated in his office that very morning, Daniel gazed out the window, his mind heavy with the weight of recent events. The suicides of Finnan and Day weighed heavily on his heart. The room felt suffocating, as if the walls themselves were closing in, reflecting the turmoil within.

Finnan's suicide by Ricin poison was understandable. He was a man whose life was over and so as not to become more of a pawn in a game that had eaten him alive, he decided to brave up and take his own life before any powerful force in the shadows did. But why Ricin? Knowing it was Ricin now, Daniel knew it was more of an assassination than a suicide.

And then there was Day, the news of Day's suicide had hit him like a physical blow. Day was not the tightest friend but he was good company. He was a proud Marxist who hated injustices in any shape or form. To an extent he made Daniel believe in the better version of himself. The one who really cared about high moral concepts like justice, fairness, goodwill without putting himself first. Now Day is declared dead by suicide. But he was assassinated like a spy.

As Daniel reflected on their lives, he decided to paint a fiction picture to connect the dots in his mind. He assumed both Finnan and Day had been drawn into the treacherous world of espionage, their paths converging with his own. They had navigated the shadows, their lives a delicate dance between loyalty and betrayal.

But while the circumstances of their deaths were intertwined with espionage, the reasons behind the desperate act of ending their lives remained shrouded in mystery. But it was just about time that they got revealed.

The more he painted, the more he realized that Finnan and Day were not victims of circumstance. But full blown perpetrators who went into this with eyes wide open. They had their ideologies in place to quell their conscience from bringing any form of cognitive dissonance in their actions. However, if they knew he was once involved why didn't they call him out too. When did not Finnan confront him during the interview? And why did Day only give him a knowing look with any further question?

Daniel pulled out from the imaginative painting and returned to his seat in his office. There was no way he could shake off the feeling that there was more that met the eye. And just like they had come for Finnan and Day, they were coming for him too. Fear gripped his bones that moment.

His face etched with lines of worry and his hands trembling slightly. The room felt suffocating, as if the walls were closing in on him. A deep sense of unease settled in the pit of his stomach, and he couldn't shake off the lingering fear that had taken hold of his mind.

As a seasoned officer, Daniel had faced danger before. He had stared down the barrel of a gun and had fought through challenging investigations. But this was different. This fear wasn't born out of physical threats or confrontations; it stemmed from an invisible force, an ominous presence lurking in the shadows. The fear of death had wrapped its icy fingers around his heart, tightening its grip that moment.

The weight of paranoia pressed heavily upon him, making him question every step he took. Every noise seemed amplified, and every shadow seemed to hold a hidden threat. The walls seemed to whisper secrets, and the creaking of the floorboards sent shivers down his spine. He couldn't escape the feeling of being watched, of being hunted.

The fear of death had always been his constant companion, following him like a dark cloud. It invaded his dreams, infusing his nights with vivid nightmares and haunting visions. His sleep had become elusive, as he found himself caught in a perpetual state of restlessness, unable to escape the clutches of his own fears.

The line between caution and paranoia blurred, and he couldn't trust his own judgement anymore. The once confident and composed officer had become a shadow of his former self, plagued by doubts and plagued by the fear of what lay ahead.

The memory of Dante Inferio's description of death seeped into his mind and the image of death formed in his mind. The eyes of Death, devoid of warmth or empathy, pierce through his soul like daggers forged from the deepest abyss.

Death held the weight of eternity, witnessing the passing of countless lives, each extinguished flame etched into their eternal memory. It sees through pretense and façade, peering into the depths of his being, laying bare the vulnerabilities and fears hidden within. It dances with a macabre grace, twisting and swirling in a sinister choreography, a relentless reminder of life's transience.

Daniel contemplated the fragility of life. He pondered the transience of existence, the fleeting nature of time, and the inevitability of death. The weight of the unknown loomed over him like a heavy shroud, intensifying his fear. He couldn't escape the constant barrage of questions that plagued his mind.

The sound of footsteps echoing in the hallway outside his office became a harbinger of danger, causing his heart to race and his palms to sweat. Each unexpected noise elicited a sharp jolt of adrenaline, as his senses heightened in a constant state of vigilance.

Daniel's eyes widened as Gilla stormed into his office, her face flushed with a mix of excitement and urgency. He had become accustomed to her spirited nature, but this time there was something different in her demeanor. He motioned for her to take a seat, his curiosity piqued.

Daniel had instructed her earlier to make inquiries from Amelia on his death and deliver a message of condolence. Gilla began recounting her visit to Finnan and

Amelia's house. She had knocked and knocked but there was no response. So she found her way in. However, as she entered the house, she couldn't find Mrs. Finnan. Instead, she stumbled upon a room where she saw a table strewn with papers and folders.

Daniel leaned forward, his eyes fixated on Gilla. She placed the files on his desk. At first he hesitated, preparing himself for what he was just about to see. He soon got his hands on them. As he flipped through them, his heart raced. The documents contained coded messages, diagrams, and photographs about the places and people that Finnan was involved with. It became clear that Finnan had been involved in something far more significant than anyone had suspected.

Gilla explained how she had taken her small camera and captured everything, ensuring they had evidence of their contents. Daniel's mind raced as he realized the implications. Finnan had indeed been entangled in a web of secrecy, and his death was not a mere suicide. It was a targeted elimination to prevent the truth from being exposed.

As Daniel studied the documents, he noticed familiar symbols and references, remnants of his own past as a Soviet spy. The realization hit him like a tidal wave. Finnan had become a pawn in a dangerous game, just as he had been all those years ago. The same forces that had driven Daniel underground and forced him to abandon his former life had now claimed Finnan's life.

Gilla's eyes were filled with a mix of concern and determination as she waited for Daniel's response. While, Daniel's mind raced, contemplating the significance of the newly discovered evidence. He knew that this discovery had the potential to change everything. It was a piece of the puzzle that could connect the dots and reveal the truth behind the deaths of Finnan and Day. But it also brought with it a wave of uncertainty and danger.

His hands trembled as he combed through the files, his eyes widening with each revelation. The evidence was mounting, pointing towards a connection between Finnan and Day that went beyond mere acquaintanceship. The clues, the cryptic messages, and the covert operations detailed within the files all hinted at the possibility that Day had been a recruit as well.

The photographs showed Finnan and Day together, sharing moments of camaraderie and trust. Their expressions were filled with a shared purpose, a hidden bond that eluded the prying eyes of others.

As he delved further into the files, Daniel discovered encrypted messages exchanged between Finnan and an unknown contact. The messages were filled with coded phrases, using covert language and disguised references. It was true after all. Day's involvement went beyond mere friendship; he was entangled in a web of espionage and intrigue.

Daniel's thoughts turned to their interactions, their conversations, and the memories of their time together. Day had always been enigmatic, guarded about his past. But now, the pieces of the puzzle began to fall into place. The moments of secrecy, the hushed conversations, and the knowing look—all took on a new significance.

The realization hit Daniel with a mix of shock and sorrow. He had known Day for years, trusted him, and confided in him. They had shared moments of laughter, of shared experiences, and of unspoken understanding. But beneath it all, there had been a hidden world of secrets, a world that Day had kept hidden even from Daniel. A world they both inhabit and play its games.

Daniel a deep breath, to remind himself he wasn't lot in a dream or figment of his imagination. This was real. His hands trembled as he sifted through the files, each document revealing a new layer of complexity to the web of intrigue. As he delved deeper, he discovered a startling revelation: Finnan's connections extended far beyond the realm of espionage. The evidence pointed to deep ties within the British police force and military ranks.

The files contained photographs, correspondence, and encrypted messages that linked Finnan to high-ranking officials and influential figures within the British establishment. There were records of clandestine meetings, covert operations, and exchanges of sensitive information. It was clear that Finnan's influence reached far beyond what Daniel had initially suspected.

The implications of these revelations were staggering. It meant that the conspiracy extended into the very heart of the institutions that were meant to uphold law and order. How deep did the roots of this network run? He wondered. And who else within the ranks of the police and military were entangled in its web?

Daniel couldn't help but feel a mixture of disbelief and outrage. The trust he had placed in the authorities had been shattered. He realized that the battle he was fighting went beyond uncovering the truth behind Finnan's death or Day's death. It was now a fight for his life.

Daniel looked over at Gilla, who had started studying the files alongside him. She stared at the evidence in disbelief. The implications of discovering ties between British police officers, military officers, and Soviet Union spies were grave and far-reaching. If these connections were proven to be true, it would signify a severe breach of national security and an erosion of trust within the country's law enforcement and defense systems. The repercussions would be nothing short of catastrophic, with the potential to plunge Britain into a state of chaos.

The revelation would shatter the public's confidence in the institutions meant to protect and serve them. The police force and the military are supposed to be on any other side that was not connected to the Soviet Union. The prime minister had vowed allegiance to the crown and their shared democracy promising to root out the seeds of communism from the nation.

Discovering that some of these individuals in high rank institutions have clandestine ties to foreign spies would not undermine the trust citizens place in these institutions, it would embolden the communist agitators and bring a spiral of intense SCEPTICISM and distrust.

The knowledge that spies had infiltrated the highest echelons of British law enforcement and defense would raise concerns about the safety and security of sensitive information. Classified intelligence, strategic plans, and operational details could have been compromised, potentially endangering national security and compromising the country's ability to defend itself against threats.

The discovery would also have severe political implications. It would ignite a crisis of confidence in the government, forcing leaders of the Union and party members to answer difficult questions about their oversight. There would be calls for investigations, resignations, and major reforms within the intelligence community and security apparatus would likely ensue, further destabilizing the political landscape.

The revelation would have a profound impact on international relations. If it became known that British police and military officers had collaborated with Soviet spies, it would severely damage Britain's reputation as a trusted ally and partner in intelligence-sharing efforts.

Other nations would question the reliability and integrity of Britain's security apparatus, potentially leading to strained diplomatic relations and a loss of crucial intelligence cooperation.

The potential consequences of such a revelation cannot be overstated. The fabric of society would be shaken, with public confidence in institutions eroded, government accountability put into question, and national security compromised. It would take significant efforts to rebuild trust, restore integrity, and ensure that such a breach could never happen again. And there could finally be the revolution that Britain had carefully avoided all these years.

Daniel's office suddenly closed in around him, a surge of fear and guilt washed over him like a tidal wave. It felt as if the weight of the world had descended upon his shoulders, threatening to crush him under its burden. His heart raced, pounding against his chest, and he struggled to catch his breath. The familiar sensation of a panic attack began to take hold. Daniel quickly stood up and rushed out of his office to get a breath of fresh air.

But Daniel was no stranger to adversity. Years of espionage and covert operations had taught him the importance of mental fortitude, of maintaining composure even in the face of overwhelming emotions. With a steely resolve, he fought against the rising tide of panic, refusing to succumb to its grip. He wouldn't allow himself to be weakened by this revelation, nor would he let Gilla see him in such a vulnerable state.

Taking deep, measured breaths, Daniel forced himself to regain control. He reminded himself of his training, of the countless dangerous situations he had faced and overcome. He summoned his inner strength, drawing upon a well of determination that had carried him through the darkest of times. Slowly, the rapid beating of his heart began to steady, and the racing thoughts in his mind began to subside.

Gathering his composure, Daniel straightened his posture and adjusted his tie. He wiped a bead of sweat from his brow and pushed back a lock of hair that had fallen onto his forehead. The lines on his face deepened, etching the weight of his experiences, but his eyes remained focused and sharp, betraying the resolute spirit within.

He knew that showing weakness was not an option, especially not now. The stakes were higher than ever, and the revelation of the extent of the conspiracy demanded unwavering strength and resolve. This wasn't about him and his survival. It's about the society he had come to love that was on the brink of falling apart.

Daniel gathered his thoughts and charted his next move. He couldn't allow himself to be consumed by fear or guilt. He would confront the darkness head-on, unearthing the secrets buried deep within the shadows.

As he walked back into his office, Daniel's facade of bravado remained intact. He greeted Gilla with a calm and composed demeanor, hiding the storm of emotions raging within. She looked at him, her eyes filled with concern. 'Are you okay sir'. But Daniel brushed off her worry with a reassuring smile, deflecting her attention from his inner turmoil.

In that moment, he made a silent promise to himself. He would protect what he cared about, and confront the demons of the past. He would unravel the web of deceit that threatened to tear his world apart. The path ahead certainly would be treacherous, but Daniel was determined to see it through, no matter the cost.

And so, with his resolve firmly in place, he set his sights on the daunting task ahead, prepared to face the challenges that lay in wait. The journey would be perilous, but there's no going back for him this time.

As the night draped its dark veil over the world, Daniel found himself once again ensnared by the grip of his restless mind. The vivid and horrific images from his dreams returned, haunting him with their eerie persistence. He lay awake, his thoughts spiraling into a labyrinth of introspection, grappling with the demons that seemed to lurk both within and without.

But he knew more than ever why those dreams came now. They were warning signs of the dangers he was about to face head on. The dangers he had avoided most of his life that had now caught up with him.

Now he knew better than running, he knew that he had delved into the darkness, willingly traversing the treacherous path of espionage. It was a world of shadows and deception, where trust was a rare commodity and betrayal lurked at every corner. He believed in a cause now, a higher purpose, something beyond himself, that justified the sacrifices and the compromises he is about to make. Yet, the weight of those choices now bore down upon him, gnawing at his soul.

His restless mind ventured further, probing the depths of his own psyche. Is this the right move to make? Was he been stupid again like the time he had fallen in love with Anna, where his decisions were out of his control and decided by an unseen powerful force beyond him?

He wondered if he was destined to forever walk this precipice between light and darkness, between duty and morality. Most of his life, each step he took, each decision he made, seemed to blur the boundaries between right and wrong. He hardly cared for morality, or God or other things but himself.

As he lay there, his mind weaving through the tapestry of his thoughts, Daniel contemplated the nature of his own existence. Was he just a pawn in a larger game, a cog in a relentless machinery that cared little for the souls it consumed? Or was there still a glimmer of humanity within him, a flickering flame that refused to be extinguished?

He earnestly yearned for peace, for respite from the turmoil that consumed him. He yearned to walk the road of redemption. He knew the road to redemption, to finding solace within his own restless soul, would be fraught with challenges. He would face the shadows and to confront the demons that lurked within the recesses of his mind. Only by facing them head-on could he hope to find some semblance of inner peace.

In the quiet of the night, as the darkness enveloped him, Daniel vowed to confront his demons, both within and without. He would delve deeper into the mysteries that surrounded him. He would call out the darkness that slimed around in the dark and face it head on. He was seeking not just the truth of the cases he investigated, but the people he knew were watching his every move seeking to larch on to him like a predator does to its prey.

And so, he closed his eyes, ready to embrace the night, the dreams, and the restlessness that awaited him. With each passing moment, he grew more determined to confront the demons and to forge a path towards redemption. He knew there lay a reward ahead in the struggle between light and darkness, between restlessness and tranquility and it is the possibility of finding a flicker of peace within him.

CHAPTER EIGHT

Daniel walked across the streets and entered the dimly lit café. He scanned the room looking for a familiar face. His eyes eventually landed on a short man with a wiry frame. He sat at a corner table, sipping his coffee. His eyes sparkled with a mischievous glint as he spotted Daniel's arrival. A smirk played on his lips, revealing his sharp wit and love for playful banter.

"Daniel Friedrich!" Gary exclaimed, and laughed. His laughter rang through the cafe. Nobody had called him Friedrich in decades. It has always been Daniel Carter ``It's been far too long." Gary continued.

It was Gary, an old friend and fellow Soviet spy from his past. They had shared many adventures together in the covert world, a bond formed by their common mission and the danger that surrounded them.

As Daniel approached, he clenched his fist. Gary was a good friend but he wished he didn't have to come around to dig up the old rotten skeleton that they had buried in the past. He couldn't help but notice the wrinkles etched on Gary's face, evidence of the years they had both lived and the secrets they had carried.

Daniel walked up to Gary and grasped his hand. He smiled back slightly at Gary’s brimming face. They settled back into their seats, the air thick with anticipation. The meeting Gary meant delving into the shadows of their past, reawakening old ghosts and unearthing buried secrets. He braced himself for the revelations that awaited.

Over steaming cups of coffee, they exchanged stories of their post-spy lives. Daniel didn't talk much as Gary did all the talking. Gary's perspective was a glorified version of events. He regaled Daniel with tales of his adventures, a mix of truth and embellishment that only he could conjure. Gary's laughter filled the air, momentarily lifting the weight of Daniel's heart slightly.

Daniel leaned back in his chair, his eyes fixed on Gary. He knew Gary would not willingly dive into serious conversation till he was done with his small talk. He was a proper Englishman to the core.

'So, Gary, tell me how life has been since you left. You seem settled, content...'

'Ah, settling down was the best decision I ever made. I traded covert operations for diaper changes and late-night storytelling. Two beautiful girls now call me "Daddy," and let me tell you, they are the light of my life.'

Daniel's eyes widened in surprise. Who married his ugly ogre and gave him children too? He thought. Even a stark blind girl knew Gary was really ugly.

'That's wonderful to hear, Gary. It is interesting how you manage to transition from the adrenaline-fueled life of a spy to passive family life.' Daniel was not sure if he was being sarcastic or passive with Gary's new life. Perhaps it was the mix of both. Maybe jealousy. Gary had something he thought he would have, and he got so close to having but lost it.

‘Yeah, it wasn't easy, I must admit.’ Gary answered as a matter of fact, ignoring Daniel's sarcasm. ‘The transition required some adjustment, yunno. But once I held my little Clara in my arms, everything changed. I tell you Daniel, the thrill of espionage is paled in comparison to the joy I found in her laughter, my little pop’s innocence. They are my reason for being.’

‘That must be quite an accomplishment,’ Daniel said softly.

‘Yea it is.’ Gary said. He chuckled mischievously, his eyes gleaming with a playful glint.

‘Ah, Daniel, I remember the days when you and Anna were quite the pair. I remember what this tall lanky guy said at your wedding...What was his name again? Vis...I could tell he had a Vis sound to his name...

'Viscount Mountbatten,' Daniel said.

'Right, Viscount Mountbatten.' Gary chuckled amused. 'I mean he was right when he said Anna had married a bullfrog in a sou'wester. I mean look at you. Almost three decades now and you've not changed at all.'

Daniel wasn't comfortable that he was now the subject of their discussion. Not only this but the subject of Anna and their divorce in the mouth of others while he was present was a no go area for him.

'Yes, just like fire and ice' Daniel replied coldly. He thought of ways to change the subject but Gary doubled down.

'Love is a complicated dance, and sometimes, no matter how hard we try, it doesn't work out. Relationships are complex, and there's always more than meets the eye.'

Now he's giving me relationship advice? Daniel thought irritatedly. 'That's rich coming from you Gary. Does your wife know about our shared history?'

Gary paused for a moment and busted into a happy laughter. 'This is a joke to you.' Daniel said still with his straight face. While Gary kept laughing

"Ah, Daniel, my friend," Gary chuckled, a twinkle in his eye. "You always were the serious one. But don't forget, laughter is our secret weapon against the darkness. I'm not a child and I obviously didn't marry one." Gary softened his laughter. 'I know you're certainly not here for banter or small talks. It has always been a pleasure of mine to irk you. From the looks of it. I was successful.' Gary leaned back to his chair and also returned Daniel's straight look. He looked quite different from the happy man that was laughing a minute earlier. Its face looked like it had a sharp form with piercing and menacing eyes that no longer held the sparkle they did earlier.

"You know, Daniel," Gary said, his tone growing softer. "We both made choices in our past, choices that led us down this path. I've got no regrets. Men, I'll do it again if I get the chance.'

'Do you mean administering Ricin to recruits who fail their task?'

'C'mon Daniel. You know I'm not that bad...'

Daniel broached the subject that had brought him here. He spoke of Finnan and Day, the connections they had discovered.

‘Ricin is either now of common use in England or they are back.’

Gary's eyes narrowed, his frowning demeanor giving way to a somber expression. He understood the gravity of the situation. They had both experienced the harsh realities of their espionage days, the consequences of their choices. The dangers they faced were not mere figments of imagination; they were very real.

"The enemy we face is formidable," Gary finally said softly, his voice carrying a hint of resignation. ‘I had nothing to do with that. You know who administers Ricin poison. Why not ask him.’ Daniel looked straight into Gary’s eyes who returned the look. There was no way he would do to Reinhardt. It had been so long and he hoped all memories of him had wiped off Reinhardt mind. Till he believed Gary. He knew what Gary was capable of doing at not doing. Still in these moments he wanted to be sure. There was hardly anyone he could trust.

'And you're not watching your back against this formidable enemy...?' Daniel asked

Gary's expression remained unwavering. He leaned back in his chair, a confident smile playing on his lips. With stunned Daniel. He was not afraid even though he had a lot to lose.

'Nah, not really, my friend. I've been out of the game for a while now. I'm not on anyone's radar anymore.' Gary chuckled 'look at me, Anita has domesticated me and fatten me up. I never took her seriously when she mentioned on our first date that she came from a long line of herdsmen. Look at me now...' Gary laughed out loud.

'What if they believe you still hold valuable information? What if they see you as a loose end?'

Gary shrugged nonchalantly, his tone laced with assurance. 'Look, I understand your concerns, but I've taken every precaution to ensure my safety. I have blended into the shadows. I'll come for them before they come for me.'

Daniel's gaze bore into Gary's, searching for any signs of uncertainty. Yet, all he saw was a steadfast resolve that spoke volumes.

My dear friend, I've paid my dues. I'm done. Fear can consume us if we let it. But I choose to live in the present, to appreciate the life I've built, and to believe in the power of redemption.'

Daniel left Gary's presence with a sense of dissatisfaction lingering in his heart. While he admired Gary's courage and optimism, he couldn't shake off the nagging feeling that there were still unanswered questions, elusive truths that remained just out of his reach.

He recalled his visit to Peter, he was also a former acquaintance in espionage like Gary. Peter had been known for his sharp intuition and wavering loyalty. But when Daniel confronted him about Finnan and Day, he received the same response as always.

But Peter had replied saying he had no clue. Daniel had believed Peter, Peter was not the most sincere person in the room but he seemed too busy concerned with other things like the brothel he was running, than to worry about running errands for a dark Soviet Lord.

Daniel had visited several other friends, some of whom had already passed away due to old age or illness. Each time, he had hoped to uncover a hidden thread of truth, a lead that would unravel the mystery shrouding Finnan and Day's deaths. But the answers eluded him, slipping through his fingers like sand.

As he arrived back home, Daniel sank into his favorite armchair, contemplating the events that had led him to this point. He stared at the television screen, the news playing in the background, but his mind was far away, lost in a sea of uncertainty. The words of Gary resonated with 'You know who administers Ricin poison. Why not ask him?' Daniel stood up from his chair, walked to his room and packed his bags.

Daniel's visit to the gothic city of Germany filled him with a mixture of dread and anticipation. Reinhardt is the only last link to his past link to his past life. A link he'll rather have nothing to do with ever in his life. Reinhardt, a man nobody dared cross or have him cross their path. His connections to the underworld ran really deep.

As he stepped off the train and entered the dimly lit streets, the oppressive atmosphere of the city weighed heavily upon him. Gothic architecture loomed overhead, casting long, eerie shadows that seemed to dance with a life of their own. The air was thick with an otherworldly energy, and whispers of dark secrets seemed to echo through the cobblestone alleyways.

Making his way through the labyrinthine streets, Daniel donned a disguise, he was quite aware of the risk of appearing bare into the city that groomed him into the intricacies of espionage. And he was well aware of the risks involved in seeking out such a dangerous individual, his former boss, the notorious espionage recruiter Reinhardt.

Reinhardt, a man with a complex past. He had fought bravely in World War II and had been one of the agitators against fascism in Germany. He firmly stood by the proponents of communism, driven by his belief in a different world order. However, the horrors of war had left an indelible mark on his heart, darkening his once hopeful spirit.

Reinhardt's recruitment approach was ruthless and cruel. The lines between right and wrong had blurred for him, and his methods had become increasingly manipulative and exploitative. Reinhardt had exploited the vulnerabilities and idealism of young men and women, seducing them with promises of a better future and a chance to fight against oppression.

Reinhardt's command gave off a charismatic yet sinister presence. And he engaged and enjoyed numerous acts of indoctrination, psychological manipulation, and a disregard for the human life of his recruit. Reinhardt had built an intricate web of spies and informants, leveraging their loyalty and commitment to further his own agenda.

Reinhardt had become obviously consumed by his own ideology, blinded to the moral consequences of his actions. The once noble cause he had fought for had been tainted by the darkness within him.

The allure of power and control had twisted his perspective, turning him into a formidable force within the world of espionage.

With every step closer to Reinhardt's mansion, Daniel braced himself for the confrontation that awaited him. He knew that facing the man who had once held power over him would be both a reckoning and a chance for redemption. The echoes of his fallen friend Day and the weight of his own guilt propelled him forward, driving him to confront the darkness head-on.

Memories of Reinhardt's training method surfaced in Daniel's mind. One particular incident stood out vividly in his mind. It was a chilling demonstration of the ruthlessness and manipulation that defined Reinhardt's approach to espionage.

In the confines of a dimly lit training room, Daniel witnessed Reinhardt orchestrating a sinister display of power. He had gathered his recruits, including a skilled spy named Alexander, to witness a lesson in the harsh realities of their chosen path. Reinhardt's intentions were clear – to instill fear and obedience in his agents, while reminding them of the consequences they might face if exposed.

With a cold, calculating demeanor, Reinhardt singled out Alexander, a promising recruit who had shown exceptional talent. He accused Alexander of being a traitor, alleging that he had betrayed their cause and shared classified information with the enemy. The room fell into a hushed silence as the weight of the accusation settled upon the young spy.

Reinhardt then took the manipulation a step further. He orchestrated a public confrontation, staging an encounter with authorities who accused Alexander of espionage. The establishment played their part convincingly, condemning Alexander and subjecting him to public humiliation and persecution. It was a cruel display meant to break the spy's spirit and to showcase the power that Reinhardt held over their lives.

As the scene unfolded, Daniel watched in horror as Alexander was subjected to relentless scrutiny, false accusations, and unwarranted persecution. The establishment wanted to make an example out of him, to send a message that those who crossed their path would meet a devastating fate.

But Reinhardt had something even more sinister in store. Reinhardt had just purchased the deadly poison Ricin the day before. It was a final act of manipulation, a chilling state to all his other recruits that the life of a spy was hung by a delicate thread, subject to the whims and schemes of those in power.

The vial was carefully wrapped up in Alexander's hands by Reinhardt right in front of everyone. 'You know what you need to do.' Reinhardt whispered into his ear. Alexander had been pushed to the brink of despair; now Reinhardt had forced him to make a choice between a painful death or the perceived shame and betrayal of the spy's life. Alexander chose the former.

As Daniel ventured into the heart of Germany, his mind was consumed by the memory of Reinhardt's ruthless training methods. The haunting image of Alexander, a skilled spy driven to the edge of despair and forced to carry the burden of a deadly poison, lingered in his thoughts.

Daniel's certainty about Reinhardt's involvement in the deaths of Finnan and Day grew with each passing moment. He knew that Reinhardt held the power and the connections to orchestrate such sinister acts. The former espionage recruiter had once held a position of authority within the spy network that produced and regulated the amount of Ricin that went out.

As Daniel journeyed towards his meeting with Reinhardt, he couldn't help but anticipate the chilling confrontation that lay ahead. He knew that questioning Reinhardt about the deaths of Finnan and Day would not be easy. He would be treading dangerous waters, challenging a man with a web of connections, secrets, and a willingness to eliminate anyone who posed a threat to his operations.

The encounter with Reinhardt was not just terrifying physically, it is also terrifying psychologically. This was Daniel facing the demon in his head-on, the darkness he had succumbed to and the treachery he once inhibited.

Daniel finally arrived at Reinhardt's secluded mansion. The imposing structure stood like a sentinel, its eerie silhouette etched against the moonlit sky. A sense of foreboding settled in the pit of Daniel's stomach, but he pushed forward.

As he entered the mansion, he was greeted by an eerie silence that enveloped the halls. The scent of old books and faded secrets permeated the air. Portraits of long-deceased ancestors lined the walls, their watchful eyes seeming to follow Daniel's every move. He couldn't shake the feeling that he was stepping into a world where darkness held sway.

Finally, he found himself standing before Reinhardt's study, a room shrouded in darkness. The door creaked open, revealing a dimly lit chamber filled with an eclectic collection of artefacts and dusty tomes. The scent of aged parchment hung in the air, intermingled with the faint aroma of cigars.

Reinhardt sat behind an ornate desk, his piercing gaze locked on Daniel. The wrinkles etched upon his face told stories of a life lived in the shadows, and his eyes held a glimmer of both cunning and weariness. The room seemed to shrink in on itself as the weight of their shared history settled upon them.

He stood up like he had been expecting Daniel and walked up to him, a small smile played on his lips. "Quite some time it has been old friend." he greeted in a strong Bavarian dialect

Daniel hesitated for a moment, staring into Reinhardt's eyes. There was a familiarity there, a connection rooted in their shared past. But behind the warmth of Reinhardt's smile, Daniel sensed the sinister undertones, the hidden agenda that lurked in the corners of that smile and pleasant greeting. He shook Reinhardt's hand, his grip firm yet tinged with unease.

"Indeed, it has been," Daniel replied in German, his voice steady.

Reinhardt's smile widened, his eyes gleaming with a mixture of amusement and something darker. "Life has a way of leading us down unexpected paths doesn't it my friend? Please, come in."

Daniel stepped into the dimly lit room, his senses heightened, attuned to every detail. He observed the sparsely furnished space, the air heavy with an enigmatic aura. Reinhardt motioned for him to take a seat, and Daniel obliged, settling into a worn leather chair that seemed to bear the weight of secrets.

As they engaged in small talk, discussing inconsequential matters, Daniel couldn't help but feel a sense of foreboding. The friendly banter masked a deeper, more sinister purpose. He knew that beneath the cordial façade, Reinhardt was a master of manipulation, adept at twisting words and orchestrating situations to his advantage.

Reinhardt's charm was undeniable, his words dripping with subtle charisma. He had a way of drawing people in, making them feel as though they were part of something greater. But Daniel had seen the darkness that lay beneath that charm, the depths to which Reinhardt would sink to achieve his goals.

Reinhardt leaned back in his chair, a sly smile curling his lips. "You've always been one to seek facts and truths and logic, Daniel," he remarked, his voice laced with an undercurrent of intrigue. "But be careful, my friend. Sometimes the truth can be more dangerous than the lies."

"I've learned that the hard way," Daniel replied, his voice tinged with a mixture of determination and caution. "Running away from danger or death gives it more power"

Reinhardt's eyes gleamed with a mixture of admiration and something darker. He leaned forward, his gaze piercing into

Daniel's soul. "Ah, that unwavering resolve," he murmured, his voice laced with a hint of menace. "It is both your greatest strength and your greatest vulnerability."

"You were always skilled at reading people, Reinhardt," Daniel retorted, his voice firm. "But I've learned a few things myself over the years."

Reinhardt chuckled, a sound that held a sinister edge. "Indeed, you have," he replied, his eyes narrowing ever so slightly. "You've learnt quite enough to settle for a life of weakness?"

Daniel's instincts urged him to be cautious. He knew Reinhardt was testing him, pushing the boundaries of their conversation to gauge his reactions. But he refused to give Reinhardt the reaction he desired.

'We both know how much you dread small talk. Why do you bore me with it now? Or have you also been domesticated like Gary?'

Daniel thought he caught a glint of surprise on Reinhardt's face. But it was a flicker of amusement that danced across Reinhardt's face. Whenever Reinhardt saw a hint of weakness in people he ate it up and ate them up with it. Daniel knew better than to have Reinhardt get the upper hand in reading him so well his fear springs out.

'Why are you here' Reinhardt finally said, happy to know where this was going

'You above all people should know why I'm here? You've always love to keep your eyes on my every move like you're obsessed. Only you can tell where the ricin that killed Finnan and day came from.'

The air in the room grew heavy with tension, an unspoken battle of wills playing out between the two men. Daniel felt a mixture of frustration and determination building within him. For a moment, the room was enveloped in silence, the weight of their words hanging in the air. Daniel's heart pounded in his chest, uncertainty mingling with determination.

Reinhardt leaned forward, his eyes gleaming with a chilling intensity. "You're walking a dangerous path, Daniel," he finally said, his voice laced with a cold certainty. "The forces at play are far greater than you can imagine. Do you truly believe you can bring them down?"

That was a tricky question, Daniel thought. It was a slippery slope. Reinhardt was avoiding the question by shooting a tougher question at Daniel. A question that any answer would give room for the weakness Reinhardt thirsted after.

‘Why are they after me?’ Daniel asked. He leaned forward, his eyes locked with Reinhardt's.

Reinhardt's smile faded, replaced by a more somber expression. The room seemed to grow colder, as if the darkness that had clouded Reinhardt's heart permeated the very air around them. ‘If they were after you’ Reinhardt placed a strong emphasis on the They ‘you won't be here questioning They.’

‘So you did it.’ Daniel's face straightened, looking deeply cold into the eyes of the cold Reinhardt. It was like staring into the eyes of death, if death loved giant-chested women and little toed feet women.

'You're aware I have a job I'm faithfully dedicated to, just like yours, right?' Reinhardt watched Daniel carefully, like he was searching for his thoughts. 'I heard you're now a journalist too. Trying to fish out your fellow comrade out for the lowlifes you work with. You have evolved to build a thick shield against shame. I like that.' Reinhardt smirked sarcastically and leaned back to his chair.

Daniel sat there quietly knowing Reinhardt had outwitted him. Reinhardt was right, he had no rights to look him in the eyes and judge him for his actions. He couldn't proceed with the conversation with why? How could you because he shared the same shadow and darkness in Reinhardt

"It seems we have reached an impasse, Daniel," Reinhardt finally said, his voice calm but tinged with a hint of mock resignation. "I wish you luck on your quest for the truth. May you find the closure you seek."

Daniel rose from his seat, his eyes leaning on anything else in the room except Reinhardt's.

As he stepped out into the dimly lit streets of Germany, Daniel felt like he had been chewed from the inside out. Reinhardt had something with words. His words not only stung but they ate through people silently.

CHAPTER NINE

Under the cover of darkness, Daniel made his way back to Reinhardt's apartment. Reinhardt might have chewed him from the inside out but he was not going to return back chewed without getting what he came from. Reinhardt already admitted he did it. But that was barely the tip of the iceberg. He held so much more to himself because he doesn't believe Daniel to be worthy enough to get those words out of his mouth.

With Reinhardt's absence at his regular uptown party, Daniel knew he had a small window of opportunity. The night swallowed him as he approached the building, careful to avoid any prying eyes. His heart raced, adrenaline coursing through his veins, as he prepared to breach Reinhardt's sanctuary.

Daniel bypassed the security measures surrounding the building. He moved swiftly, his movements calculated and silent, leaving no trace of his intrusion. With each step closer to Reinhardt's apartment, his determination grew, overriding any reservations he may have had.

Finally, he stood before the door, his gloved hand hovering over the lock. The weight of his actions settled upon him, the gravity of his decision to trespass upon Reinhardt's privacy. But the nagging suspicion, the need for answers, pushed him forward.

Taking a deep breath, Daniel picked the lock with deft precision. The door swung open soundlessly, revealing a glimpse into Reinhardt's private world. He stepped inside, the darkness of the apartment enveloping him, the only source of illumination coming from the faint glow of the moon through the windows.

Daniel's footsteps were measured and cautious as he made his way through the apartment. He was careful not to disturb the meticulous order that Reinhardt seemed to maintain. Each room he entered held a sense of Reinhardt's personality; dread and death.

Soon, Daniel's heart raced as he glanced towards the corner of the room where Reinhardt's dogs slept; two female giant German Shepherds. He knew that any sudden movement or noise could alert them and jeopardize his mission.

With careful precision, Daniel stepped lightly, his movements fluid and controlled. He focused on maintaining a calm demeanor, avoiding any sudden gestures that might startle the slumbering beasts. Every muscle in his body tensed as he tiptoed past them, his senses heightened to detect even the faintest sound.

He had studied the dogs during his previous visit, observing their habits and reactions. Now, that knowledge served him well as he navigated the room with utmost caution. He moved with a slow and deliberate grace, mindful of the creaking floorboards that could betray his presence.

As he neared the dogs, Daniel held his breath, his eyes fixed on their peaceful forms. He could feel the weight of their presence, the latent energy coursing through their bodies. It was a delicate dance, a test of his agility and control.

With a silent prayer, Daniel inched past the dogs, using his peripheral vision to keep track of their positions. He adjusted his path, maneuvering around them without brushing against their slumbering bodies. It was a nerve-wracking task, every step measured and calculated.

Time seemed to stretch as he passed through the room, his movements akin to a ghost in the night. He couldn't afford to make a single mistake. The consequences could be dire, not just for himself, but for his mission.

Finally, with bated breath, Daniel emerged on the other side of the room, having successfully traversed the treacherous path without rousing the sleeping giants.

Relief washed over him, mingling with a sense of accomplishment.

The study proved to be the most promising location for his search. It was there that Reinhardt kept his most precious possessions, his secrets hidden within the depths of the room. Daniel scanned the shelves, his fingers brushing against the spines of books that concealed more than just knowledge.

He found himself drawn to a particular volume, its worn cover betraying its significance. With a sense of anticipation, he pulled it from the shelf, his eyes scanning the pages for any hidden notes or clues. But as he turned each page, disappointment washed over him. The book held no revelations, no answers to the questions that haunted him.

Moving from room to room, Daniel's search intensified. Drawers were discreetly opened, papers meticulously examined, and hidden compartments probed. But the apartment revealed no secrets, no smoking gun that would expose Reinhardt's true intentions.

As he stood in Reinhardt's bedroom, a sense of defeat washed over him. The silence of the room echoed his disappointment. Had Reinhardt truly managed to erase all traces of his dark dealings? Or was Daniel simply not looking in the right places?

He ran back to Reinhardt’s study to be sure he checked well. Suddenly, his eyes landed on a locked safe nestled within Reinhardt's study. The sight sent a surge of anticipation through Daniel's veins. He knew that if there was any place where Reinhardt would keep damning evidence, it would be there.

Pulling out his trusty tools, Daniel set to work, his hands steady despite the adrenaline coursing through his veins. With expert precision, the lock yielded, and the safe door swung open, revealing its long-held secrets.

Inside, Daniel found a collection of documents. The first document he examined contained detailed plans outlining the administration of Ricin to England. As he continued to sift through the documents, his hands trembling slightly, he stumbled upon a collection of photographs. Finnan and Day. The photos were stamped with the chilling word "Executed," marking the tragic end of their lives.

Daniel's eyes widened as he stumbled upon another set of documents within the safe. These papers revealed a sinister connection that extended beyond the poisoning plot. They contained the names and photographs of British police and military officers who were involved in Soviet espionage. They were just like the ones Gilla had brought to him in the office.

While going through these files. His eyes caught sight of a folder with his own name on it. Curiosity mingled with apprehension as he pulled it out from the stack. With trembling hands, he opened the folder to reveal a compilation of information about himself—his past, his accomplishments, and even details from his personal life.

A mix of confusion and unease washed over Daniel as he scanned through the contents of the file. How had Reinhardt obtained such intimate knowledge about him? The realization that he had been under thorough surveillance struck him with a jolt. He knew Reinhardt had maintained keeping an eye on him after he left, but he never thought it was this intense. It was as if he had been laid bare, exposed to the prying eyes of a man who could switch up for death itself.

Photographs of Daniel filled the file, capturing him in various mundane moments of his life. He saw images of himself walking down crowded streets, sitting in cafes engrossed in conversation, and even captured in the intimacy of his own home. He found reports documenting his activities, conversations he had deemed private, and details about his personal relationships.

However, amidst the unsettling revelations, there was one lingering question that hung in the air: Was he the next target of the Ricin poisoning? The evidence in the file was inconclusive, leaving him on edge. Yet, the pieces began to fall into place. The Soviet spy group wanted him back. They saw him as a valuable asset, someone they couldn't afford to lose.

The implications were daunting. It became clear that his pursuit of the truth had put him directly in the crosshairs of dangerous adversaries. The sinister plot to administer Ricin to England was just one layer of a much larger scheme, and Daniel had inadvertently become entangled in its web.

Daniel's heart raced as he stumbled upon another file that had a big bold CONFIDENTIAL written on it. He opened and it revealed that the next target of the assassination plot was none other than the Prime Minister of England, along with a member of the royal family. The gravity of the situation intensified, and a sense of urgency washed over him.

His mind raced, contemplating the implications of this new revelation. The thought of such a heinous act sent shivers down his spine. Lives hung in the balance, and the responsibility to prevent this catastrophic event fell squarely on his shoulders.

In the midst of the chaos of shocking revelations and thoughts, Daniel's mind began to formulate a plan. He needed to gather all the evidence he needed. Daniel's heart pounded in his chest as he hastily made his way out of Reinhardt's apartment, clutching the files that contained crucial information about the assassination plot. The adrenaline surged through his veins, fueling his determination to expose the truth and protect the lives of the Prime Minister and the royal family.

With a sense of urgency, Daniel hailed a taxi and jumped into the backseat. The city lights blurred past, creating a disorienting backdrop to his racing thoughts. He was heading to the airport first thing in the morning.

Daniel recounted the chilling details he had discovered to Mason and Graham. The room fell into a heavy silence as the weight of the information settled upon them.

Mason furrowed his brow, absorbing the gravity of the situation while Graham, the analytical mind in the room, leaned forward, his eyes filled with both concern and curiosity. They exchanged glances, acknowledging the severity of what they were about to confront.

Daniel's voice was filled with a mix of urgency and determination as he laid out the evidence before them. He revealed the names, the photographs, and the intricate connections that tied the British police and military officers to the Soviet espionage network. He described the plan to administer Ricin to England, the execution of Finnan and Day, and the targeted assassination of the Prime Minister and the royal family.

Mason's face hardened, his eyes flickering with anger. "This shit’s running longer than I can ever imagine to be" he muttered, his voice laced with frustration. "We need to assemble a task force, a team we can trust implicitly. We must work discreetly, carefully vetting every individual involved in this investigation. Lives depend on it."

Graham sat still on his desk. His eyes still resting on the file "We'll need to secure additional evidence, gather more intelligence, and establish a network of reliable sources," he finally said, his voice brimming with purpose.

'We've got all the evidence here Graham, it's evident we need to act fast.'

Graham looked up to Mason with a glare. 'You can go ahead and skip all necessary protocol in your imagination but we aren't going anywhere with that. We will act, but we can't overact. We need to ensure the right people are brought to justice.'

'We need to be cautious. We're walking on a treacherous path, and the enemies we face will stop at nothing to protect their secrets." Graham concluded

Daniel nodded, acknowledging the necessity of discretion. As he stepped out of the office, a curious sensation washed over him—a momentary tranquility amidst the chaos that surrounded him. It was a moment of unexpected peace, one that seemed to quell the fear of death lurking within him.

A calm descended upon Daniel's restless mind. It was as if the weight of the world had momentarily lifted from his shoulders, and he found solace in the midst of uncertainty. The knowledge that he had allies and the promise of support from Mason and Graham brought a sense of reassurance, reminding him that he was not alone in this dangerous endeavor.

He drifted into his lucid dreaming again. The internal turmoil that had plagued him since uncovering the file momentarily subsided, replaced by a rare moment of clarity. He appreciated that his mission went beyond personal survival—it was about protecting the innocent, ensuring justice, and preserving the society that he had come to love.

As he walked through the bustling streets, a soft breeze brushed against his face, carrying with it a sense of serenity. The noise of the city seemed to fade into the background, replaced by a quiet calm that enveloped him. It was a moment of respite, where the fears and dangers that loomed ahead momentarily receded.

The realization that death could be a possible outcome of his pursuit no longer stirred panic or trepidation within him. Instead, a newfound acceptance settled in, a resolute understanding that the cause he fought for was worth the risks. The serenity he felt was rooted in his unwavering commitment to do what was right, regardless of the personal cost.

In that moment of peace, Daniel embraced the impermanence of life, acknowledging that his actions might shape a better future, even if he wasn't there to witness it. The fear of death faded into the background, replaced by a profound sense of purpose and an unwavering determination to protect those who couldn't protect themselves.

Daniel shook himself off the dream and walked back to his office. He found Gilla in the office, engrossed in her work. He approached her with a sincere expression, Gilla had been of great help to him all throughout this case and he couldn't help but feel stings of guilt that he had underestimated her and looked down on her abilities.

He cleared his throat, catching her attention, and she looked up, surprise flickering across her face. "Gilla, I owe you an apology," Daniel began, his voice filled with genuine remorse. "I...well to put it likely, I have been a jerk, dismissing your capabilities and not giving you the credit you deserve. I want to acknowledge the valuable contribution you have made to this case."

Gilla looked at him, a mixture of surprise and cautious hope in her eyes. She had faced his dismissive attitude before, and his unexpected change of heart took her aback. She remained silent, allowing him to continue.

"I've realized that I've been blind to the talent and dedication you bring to the table," Daniel continued, his voice earnest. "You have been relentless in your pursuit of the truth, and I truly appreciate your efforts. Without your assistance, we wouldn't have made the progress we have in uncovering the secrets surrounding Finnan and Day."

Gilla's expression softened, and she nodded, the tension in her shoulders easing slightly. She had longed for this recognition, yearning for a partnership built on respect and equality.

"I'm sorry for underestimating you and for not valuing your skills and insights," Daniel continued, his tone sincere. "You are an asset to this investigation, and I want to assure you that moving forward, I will treat you as an equal partner. We...I need each of your strengths to navigate the complexities of this case." Daniel sighed. A sense of gratitude washing over him. He realized the significance of having Gilla's support and expertise by his side. It was a collaboration that had the potential to yield powerful results.

"I accept your apology, Daniel," Gilla finally spoke, with a curvy smile on her face. "I believe in the importance of teamwork and trust in solving cases. We have a long road ahead of us, and I hope we can move forward as friends"

"Thank you, Gilla," he said sincerely.

‘So, I've been wondering about something. You've mentioned that you've travelled quite a bit, but you never really mentioned where you're from. Care to share?’

Gilla pauses for a moment ‘Well, Daniel, I suppose I've never really had a single place that I could call home. I've lived in different countries and moved around quite a bit. Let's just say I've had a rather unconventional upbringing.’

‘I see. A woman of mystery, then?’ Daniel smiled.

‘You could say that. I've learned to adapt and embrace the unknown. It keeps life interesting, wouldn't you agree?’

As much as he saw Gilla every day he could help but be intrigued by her enigmatic persona. He had never found her as interesting as he did that moment. Like Anna, she has a thing with words that made him want to hear more. Even if it’s something he had no interest in.

‘Thank you, Gilla.’ he finally said. ‘It hasn't been an easy journey, but knowing that you’ve got my back gives me confidence.’

Gilla smiled, looking down at the files she had at hand.

Silence rested in the room for a while. Gilla kept her eyes on her file. While Daniel looked around his office awkwardly thinking of what to say. ‘Want to go on a walk?’ Gilla asked. Daniel nodded.

They walked through the bustling streets of London, their conversation intertwined with determination and a shared purpose. The city lights illuminated their path, radiating with the ease the air brought. In the midst of their banter, Daniel, in a rare moment, curiously poked further asking Gilla about her love life.

‘Ah, love... It's a complex and unpredictable thing, isn't it?’ Gilla said giggling. ‘I had a boyfriend who was absolutely infatuated with motorcycles. He loved his bike more than anything else.

Daniel smiled knowingly, knowing where this was going.

‘He decided to take me for a ride on his prized motorcycle, one day. I was both excited and nervous, you know, I mean I was a teenager, what do you expect? Let's just say I spent the rest of the day getting mud off my hair and nursing a giant painful swell at my rear end.'

Daniel chuckled.

'I remember sitting there, covered in mud, trying to hold back my laughter as my boyfriend panicked and tried to clean me up. It was more embarrassing than anything else.

Daniel chuckled a little more. If he had had a daughter with Anna, she would probably be around the age of Gilla. That moment he imagined he had those things he wanted with her that he never got.

'I learnt not to take things too seriously at that moment. I took a break from love.'

As the evening settled in, their laughter echoed through the streets of London. There was a sense of camaraderie and connection in the air. It was a moment where the weight of their investigations and the dangers they faced seemed momentarily lifted. It was a reminder that amidst the chaos and uncertainty, finding joy and humor can be a source of strength.

CHAPTER TEN

Daniel's restlessness began to consume him once again in the next few days, but this time it carried an added weight—a heavy blanket of depression that enveloped his being. The uncertain future ahead weighed heavily on his shoulders. Was he going to make it out alive or dead in this game? This dragged him deeper into the abyss of despair.

Days turned into sleepless nights as his mind became a battleground of conflicting emotions. The vivid horrors from his dreams invaded his waking thoughts, intertwining with the harsh reality of his circumstances. He struggled to find solace in the activities that once brought him joy, as the darkness within seemed to overshadow everything else.

The weight of depression pressed upon his chest, making each breath a laborious task. The world around him appeared muted, devoid of color and vitality. It felt as though he was trapped in a never-ending cycle of despair, unable to find respite from the turmoil that plagued his mind and soul.

The once vibrant streets of London became mere corridors of shadows, the laughter and chatter of people passing by serving as a constant reminder of the disconnect he felt. It was as if he existed in a parallel universe, separated from the normalcy and happiness that others seemed to effortlessly embrace.

The weight of depression manifested in physical sensations—a perpetual fatigue that settled in his bones, a heaviness in his limbs that made every step a struggle. The simplest tasks became monumental challenges, and the energy required to face each day seemed insurmountable. It was a constant battle between his will to keep going and the suffocating grip of despair.

In the solitude of his thoughts, Daniel questioned his purpose and wondered if his pursuit of truth and justice was worth the toll it took on his mental and emotional well-being. The relentless pursuit of answers and the constant exposure to danger had taken its toll, eroding his spirit and leaving him feeling lost and vulnerable.

He longed for a moment of respite, a glimmer of light to pierce through the darkness. But in the depths of his depression, it felt as though hope was an elusive mirage, always just out of reach. The weight of his own thoughts threatened to consume him, whispering doubts and insecurities that amplified his despair.

Isolation became both a refuge and a prison. Sleep, once a respite from the waking world, became entangled in the grip of depression. Nights were marked by restless tossing and turning, plagued by haunting dreams and a restless mind. The darkness that clouded his days seeped into his nights, eroding the sanctuary of rest and replacing it with restless torment.

Daniel's battle with depression was further compounded by the nagging fear that loomed over him—the haunting notion that he was being hunted by the very forces he had dedicated his life to unravelling. The fear of assassination, of becoming a target for those he had once pursued, cast a chilling shadow over his every thought and action.

Every unexpected sound, every unfamiliar face, sent a shiver down his spine, igniting the adrenaline-fueled fight-or-flight response within him. The weight of paranoia settled upon his shoulders, tightening its grip with each passing day. It was a constant, gnawing presence that whispered sinister possibilities into his mind.

The knowledge that he possessed damning information, that he had stumbled upon secrets that threatened the powerful and the dangerous, fueled his anxiety. He became hyper aware of his surroundings, constantly scanning for any signs of surveillance or suspicious activity. Every stranger became a potential threat, and every interaction carried an undercurrent of suspicion.

It was in these moments that Daniel decided he would take his own life. It wasn't an emotional despair that sprung forth from the despair he felt. It was a practical and logical destination he had thoroughly thought out well and intended to execute properly. It was an act of bravery for him like the Samaria in Japanese oral tradition. He would take his life before people like Reinhardt laid their hands on him and whisk him into the dark without any thought or remorse.

Daniel got his gun he used for hunting deers in the field close to his house and prepared himself for his final minute on earth. He thought of saying a prayer but sounded unlikely. If there was a God all these while then his prayers were useless. He deserved to be in hell with the cloud he had led there. While Daniel contemplated this. He heard a knock on the door.

Daniel walked up to the door and opened to find Mary, standing there with a warm smile. He wasn’t expecting her, but couldn't tell if he was pleased about this impromptu visit or not.

He made way for her to come in, while Mary matched carefully into the house.

I heard you've been locked in here for days. I thought to bring in some air, well, and some fresh pastries. Thought you could use a pick-me-up. ``

Daniel remained quiet as Mary brought her pastries to his face. They did smell nice. Perhaps a little bit of this delicious goodness would be the perfect parting memory for him.

Mary went straight to the kitchen and made a cup of coffee. She brought Daniela and her cup to him and they both sat in his living room sipping on steaming cups of coffee and nibbling on the pastries quietly.

Mary leaned in closer to Daniel, she glanced around cautiously, almost in a comical fashion, her voice dropping to a hushed tone. "Daniel, I have something to tell you. Something... rather peculiar that I've noticed recently."

Daniel's eyes raised from the coffee mug like he had just emerged from the trance the delicious coffee took him into. "What's that?"

Mary took a deep breath and continued, "Well, I've been observing Gilla for a while now, and there have been some strange occurrences that I can't help but find suspicious. Just the other day, I happened to walk by your office, and I saw Gilla inside, searching through your files as if she was looking for something specific."

‘Maybe she was just organizing or looking for a document related to our ongoing investigation." Daniel replied tiredly. He was a little disappointed that this took a quick gossipy turn.

Mary shook her head, her eyes filled with certainty. "It didn't seem that way, Daniel. The look on her face was frantic, almost as if she was in a hurry to find something and didn't want anyone to know. It didn't sit right with me."

Daniel furrowed his brow and sighed deeply. He remained quiet. Not because he didn't have anything to say but he felt tired saying it. Besides, he wanted a private moment with his coffee.

"I just thought you should know, Daniel. It's always best to be aware of any potential irregularities, especially given the delicate nature of our work." Mary continued. She nodded, a hint of worry in her eyes.

Mary shifted nervously in her seat, her gaze fixed on Daniel who was still quiet. "I'm just saying, Daniel, there's something off about Gilla. I can't put my finger on it, but I've noticed some peculiar behaviour."

Daniel sighed, and finally said. "Mary, we've been working with Gilla for years. She's been loyal and dedicated. I think you might be reading too much into things."

Mary's eyes narrowed slightly, a hint of frustration evident in her voice. "I understand your trust in her, but I can't ignore what I've seen. It's not just this one incident. There have been other instances that make me question her intentions."

Daniel was silent.

"Well, for starters, I overheard her talking to someone on the phone, speaking in hushed tones and sounding rather secretive," Mary replied, her voice lowering as she leaned closer to Daniel. "It makes me wonder who she was conversing with and what they were discussing."

'She is more of a private person, Mary. Don't overthink this.'

Mary shook her head, her expression determined. "I wish it were that simple, Daniel. But there's more. I've seen her sneaking glances at you when she thinks no one is watching. It's as if she's hiding something, and it's unsettling."

Daniel sighed, growing weary of the conversation. "Mary, I think you might be letting your personal feelings get in the way. I trust her, and I need you to trust her too."

Mary sunk into silence. He wasn't thinking she is jealous of Gilla, is he? "You think this is about jealousy? Daniel,' Mary said 'I've always had your best interests at heart. I wouldn't bring this up if I didn't genuinely believe there was something going on."

Daniel's tone turned firmer, his voice laced with a touch of frustration. "That's enough Mary," he sighed. 'I don't need any rift stirring up at this moment of my life.'

Mary's face flushed with a mix of anger and disappointment. "I'm not trying to cause trouble, Daniel. I just thought you should know. You've always trusted me to be honest, and I'm only trying to fulfil that trust."

"Mary, I understand your intentions, and I appreciate your loyalty. But right now, I need you to focus on...' Fuck it. Daniel thought and stood up. Whoever said nagging women could make a man end his own life was right.

Daniel stood up 'I need to get a game in the field.' Daniel said leaving with his gun in his hands. This was the perfect push he needed to decide he didn't want to leave again, he thought as he matched off to the field, leaving Mary behind in his house.

The cool breeze brushed against his face, he could hear the echoes of the afterlife in them. Suddenly, life seems spiritual. The trees spoke to him and hidden shadowy figures sprung out of the forest to accompany him on the journey of death.

As he ventured deeper into the field, his anticipation grew. Death, his close friend that watched him in the shallows beckoned to him slowly and quietly. It was a melody of darkness and despair. Still, he relished the solitude. Alone he came. Alone he goes. From dust to dust from ash to ash.

He got to the thick of the forest and reached for his gun to load a bullet, an unsettling realization washed over him. His hand grazed the empty space where the bullet should have been. Daniel's eyes widened in disbelief. How could he have forgotten such a crucial element on this journey to the afterlife?

Pissed with himself, frustration welled up within him. He cursed under his breath, berating his absentmindedness. How could he have been so careless? The implications of his oversight echoed in his mind.

Daniel turned on his heels and retraced his steps back to the house. Each stride was fueled by a mix of annoyance and urgency. He couldn't fathom the idea of returning to the field of death replaying the deeply meaningful transcendental things he had just witnessed.

The journey back to the house felt longer than before, each passing second amplifying his impatience. The distant sound of his footsteps echoed in his ears, a constant reminder of his own fallibility. Yet, he remained resolute, unwilling to let his own oversight derail his mission.

When Daniel got to his house, his heart pounded in his chest as he stood at the entrance of his house, staring at the bullet-ridden walls. Fear and shock coursed through his veins, his mind struggling to comprehend the scene before him. With trembling steps, he cautiously entered the house, his eyes scanning the room for any signs of life.

His worst fears were realized when he saw Mary's lifeless body slumped in the chair he had left her. The sight struck him like a lightning bolt, sending waves of grief and disbelief crashing over him. A mixture of horror and sorrow gripped his soul, and for a moment, he was paralyzed by the weight of the tragedy that had unfolded in his own home.

Rushing to Mary's side, Daniel knelt down, his hands trembling as he touched her lifeless form. Her once vibrant eyes were now empty, her smile forever frozen. The realization of her untimely death pierced through him, filling him with an indescribable sense of loss. He couldn't comprehend how? Why? What had she done to deserve such fate?

A storm of emotions surged within him. Grief mingled with guilt as Daniel blamed himself for living her behind in the house. Anguish weighed heavily on Daniel's shoulders as he realized that the danger had come knocking at his own doorstep. The sinister forces he had been investigating had breached the sanctity of his home, leaving a trail of devastation in their wake.

With a heavy heart, Daniel gently closed Mary's eyes, offering a silent prayer for her soul. He knew that her death would forever be etched in his memory, a painful reminder of the stakes involved in his pursuit of truth.

Leaving Mary's lifeless body behind, Daniel stepped out of the house, his eyes blurred with unshed tears. The weight of grief settled upon his shoulders, threatening to engulf him in a sea of sorrow. It had been a long time since he had allowed himself to feel so deeply, to let the raw emotions rise to the surface. The loss of Mary, an innocent soul caught in the crossfire of his dangerous world, pierced his heart with a profound sadness.

Memories of their interactions flooded his mind—their conversations, the laughter they had shared, the genuine friendship they had forged. Mary had been a steady presence in his life, a loyal confidante who had believed in him even when he struggled to believe in himself. The void she left behind was immense, a void that could never be filled.

A single tear escaped Daniel's eye, tracing a path down his cheek. He couldn't help but think of all the moments they would never share again, the laughter and camaraderie forever lost. The weight of regret settled upon his heart, regret for not being able to protect her, for unknowingly involving her in the dangerous game he had been playing.

The tears soon began to pour and pour till found himself sobbing deeply. The evening sun melted into the darkness, fleeing the soreness and sting of the scene.

CHAPTER ELEVEN

The next few days Daniel hid in the darkness. Hiding became his refuge, a means to protect himself from the unseen threats that lurked in the shadows. The realization that he was next, that the same fate that had befallen Mary could soon befall him, ignited a primal instinct within him to survive.

He knew that the forces at play were powerful, elusive, and ruthless. They had already taken lives and left a trail of destruction in their wake. Daniel couldn't ignore the weight of their presence, the ever-present threat that loomed over him. Every creaking floorboard, every rustling leaf outside his window, sent shivers down his spine, reminding him of the danger that lurked just beyond his reach.

In his self-imposed exile, Daniel sought solace in the shadows. He became a ghost, vanishing into the depths of anonymity. Gone were the days of predictable routines and open vulnerability. He carefully erased his footprint, severed ties with former acquaintances, and adopted new identities in a bid to obscure his trail.

The once bustling city streets, once familiar and comforting, now felt like a labyrinth of potential dangers. He moved with caution, eyes darting from shadow to shadow, hyper aware of his surroundings. He sought hidden corners and abandoned safe houses, seeking temporary respite in the crevices of the world where he could remain invisible to prying eyes.

Each passing day brought a heightened sense of paranoia. He questioned every encounter, every friendly smile, wondering if they were mere disguises concealing sinister intentions. Trust became a luxury he could no longer afford, as he grappled with the knowledge that the enemy could be anyone—friend, foe, or stranger.

The isolation weighed heavily upon Daniel's soul. The walls of his hidden sanctuary became both his fortress and his prison. Loneliness wrapped around him like a suffocating cloak, reminding him of the sacrifices he had made and the depths to which he had descended to protect himself.

The fear of being hunted consumed him, gnawing at his sanity like a relentless predator.
Hiding became Daniel's refuge, a means to protect himself from the unseen threats

that lurked in the shadows. The realization that he was next, that the same fate that had befallen Mary could soon befall him, ignited a primal instinct within him to survive.

And so, he waited, his heart beating with a mix of anxiety and hope, hoping that the moment to step out of the shadows and reclaim his life was fast approaching. He had gotten a covert message from Gilla during the day. He was told to go to a phone booth at a nearby hostel so she could speak with him

After waiting for an hour for the phone to ring, Daniel's heart skipped a beat as the phone finally rang, breaking the suffocating silence that had enveloped him. With trembling hands, he answered the call, his voice barely steady as he spoke.

"Gilla?" he said, his voice laced with a mixture of relief and concern. "Is that you?"

"Yes, Daniel," Gilla's voice came through, a mixture of urgency and fear. "I need to see you. It's urgent."

A surge of emotions flooded Daniel's senses. Relief washed over him, knowing that Gilla was still alive, but his worry intensified at the thought of what she might have experienced.

"Are you safe?" Daniel asked, his voice filled with genuine concern. "Where are you?"

"I managed to escape," Gilla replied, her voice filled with anxiety. "But I can't stay here. It's not safe. We need to meet."

Daniel's mind raced, contemplating the best course of action. He knew that meeting Gilla could be a risk. But he knew he could keep hiding forever.

"Where are you Gilla?'

'My grandpa's house in the countryside. They can't find us there.' Gilla shared the address information with Daniel and hung up.

Daniel's mind buzzed with a mix of anticipation and contemplation as he embarked on the journey to Gilla's grandfather's house. The road stretched out before him, winding through the picturesque countryside, as if mirroring the twists and turns of his own life. The landscape whizzed by, but his thoughts remained fixated on his next move.

As he navigated the familiar yet unfamiliar roads, a sense of unease settled in his chest. The weight of the world pressed upon him, and he found himself questioning the choices that lay ahead. Should he truly embrace the safety and solace offered by Gilla's family haven? Or was it merely another temporary respite, a fleeting illusion of security?

That moment, the images of Mary's lifeless body flashed before his eyes, a haunting reminder of the stakes involved. The fear that gripped him tightened its hold, threatening to consume him entirely. He accelerated the wheels of his car to spin faster, carrying him closer to the refuge offered by Gilla's grandfather.

As he neared his destination, a sense of calm washed over him. The air seemed to still, as if the universe itself held its breath in anticipation of what lay ahead. The road curved, revealing a hidden path that led to the haven he sought. Gilla's grandfather's house appeared before him, nestled in a tranquil embrace of nature.

Stepping out of the car, Daniel embraced serenity that enveloped the surroundings. The beauty of the landscape whispered promises of tranquility and renewal. With a deep breath, he crossed the threshold, entering a world untouched by the chaos that had defined his recent days.

The English countryside, with its rolling hills, picturesque landscapes, and quaint villages, is a place of tranquil beauty and idyllic charm. In this rural oasis, nestled amongst nature's embrace, stood a house that seemed frozen in time. It sat peacefully in solitude, its exterior weathered by the passage of years and the whims of seasons.

The house stood as a testament to the architectural heritage of the region. Its stone walls, sturdy and weathered, exuded a sense of permanence and timelessness. Moss and ivy crept along the aged facade, as if nature herself sought to reclaim the man-made structure. The touch of green against the weathered stone added a touch of vibrancy to the otherwise muted palette.

A gravel pathway, once meticulously maintained, now lay partially overgrown, its surface scattered with fallen leaves and the imprints of nature's creatures. The crunch underfoot echoed through the quiet air, offering a soundtrack to the visitor's exploration. The path led to the front door, its wood worn and faded, displaying the years of use and neglect. It stood there, a portal into the mysteries that lay beyond.

As Daniel approached the house, the scent of earth and foliage filled the air, mingling with the gentle breeze that rustled through the surrounding trees. The sound of chirping birds and distant rustling leaves created a symphony of nature, enveloping the house in a serene aura. It was a refuge from the chaos of urban life, a sanctuary where one could find solace and a connection with the land.

The garden, once a vibrant tapestry of colors, now bore signs of untamed wilderness. Wildflowers stubbornly sprouted amidst overgrown grass, their delicate petals swaying in the wind. Unpruned shrubs and bushes seemed to form a protective barrier around the house, creating a natural screen that shielded it from prying eyes.

The house looked empty and devoid of human presence. Yet Daniel stepped across the threshold of the quiet and empty house, an eerie stillness settled around him. The air felt stagnant, devoid of life and activity. Every creak of the floorboards seemed amplified, echoing through the empty rooms, heightening his senses and stirring his intuition.

His eyes scanned the surroundings while the silence pressed upon Daniel, urging him to listen to the unspoken cues that prickled at his skin. He couldn't shake the feeling that something was amiss.

Moving cautiously into the house, he found the living room to be a stud. The musty scent of old paper lingered in the air, adding a layer of nostalgia to the atmosphere. His gaze focused on a book, seemingly out of place, partially hidden beneath a layer of dust.

Suddenly out from the door behind him emerged three menacing giant looking men in black suits. Their cold gazes bore into him, radiating an aura of danger and hostility.

His mind raced, searching for a way out of this perilous situation. But as he scanned the room, his worst fears were realized. Three additional men in black had silently infiltrated the house, effectively cutting off his retreat. The odds were stacked against him, and he could feel the walls of the room closing in, suffocating him with their presence.

With a steady resolve, Daniel assessed his surroundings. He noted the windows, the furniture, and the limited options for escape. The room itself became both his shield and his prison, offering him cover from the menacing individuals while simultaneously limiting his freedom.

The tension in the air grew palpable as a silent standoff ensued. The men took hold of Daniel and tied him to a wooden chair. Daniel fought to free himself from the ropes. He heard footstep walk up to the room and lifted up his eyes. Emerging from one of the rooms in the house were Reinhardt and Gilla.

Gilla stood before him as a confederate to Reinhardt. While Reinhardt, wearing a self-satisfied smirk, approached Daniel with an air of authority. His eyes gleamed with a mixture of triumph and malice, reveling in the chaos he had orchestrated. It became clear to Daniel that Reinhardt had masterminded the entire situation, manipulating events to ensnare him within the intricate trap.

Gilla's cold and disdainful gaze pierced through Daniel, leaving him with a profound sense of emptiness. The silence that hung in the air spoke volumes, the absence of words conveying a deeper betrayal than any verbal confrontation could express. Their shared moments, their trust, and their connection had all been reduced to nothing more than a facade.

Reinhardt's voice cut through the tension, his tone dripping with satisfaction. "The old little bird wants to fly away...' he said looking at Gilla.

Daniel's heart ached as he absorbed Gilla's cold demeanor, a mix of anger, hurt, and confusion swirled within Daniel. He wanted answers, an explanation or something. How could she stand there, her gaze filled with disdain, without uttering a single word?

Reinhardt's smirk faltered for a moment, "You're a fool, Daniel," he retorted. "You think you can outsmart us? You're just a pawn."

The room fell into an eerie silence as the standoff continued. The weight of the unspoken words, the unspoken truths, hung heavily in the air. Daniel knew that the road ahead would be treacherous, fraught with danger and uncertainty. But he also knew that he had to press forward, to uncover the secrets that had been hidden from him and to confront the darkness that had infiltrated his life.

As he glanced at Gilla one final time, a mix of sadness and determination filled his gaze. He silently vowed to himself that he would uncover the truth behind her betrayal, even if it meant walking a path fraught with heartache and betrayal. The journey ahead would be difficult, but

Daniel was no longer the naive pawn he had once been. He had become a player in this dangerous game, ready to face whatever challenges awaited him in his quest for justice and redemption.

'Let me go, Reinhardt!' Daniel said struggling against the ropes.

'I will in a minute. We need to talk about some business while we are at it.' Reinhardt said smirking

Reinhardt grabbed a vial of Ricin from the table it was seated on. He look from the poison to Daniel with a sinister smile on his face. 'You're thinking what I'm thinking?' he said. He dropped the veil on the table, got a nearby chair, pulled it closer to Daniel and sat face to face with Daniel.

‘We need your help. And by we I don’t mean myself.’ Reinhardt chuckled slightly. ‘I mean I, Gilla, Graham and...well many others you don’t need to know right now.’

Daniel’s widened at the mention of Graham’s name.

‘Oh, you didn’t know he was with us? Sorry about that.’ Reinhardt rich German English accent seem to blend quietly into a Scottish accent. That was Reinhardt, he was unpredictable and filled with so many personalities.

‘You above anyone else knew about that greater good we chase, regardless of the prices we have to pay in the process. We don’t look back. We only keep going. But you acted cowardly Daniel. You looked back.’

He looked up to Gilla who was still staring Daniel down. 'She's a sweet one Dan.' Reinhardt resumed his Bavarian Germanic accent. 'She asked me to save your life that you could prove useful to execute our goals. Don't mess things up for her Dan.'

'Here are your options, Daniel.' Reinhardt continued in English. 'You can either choose to meet the same fate as Finnan and Day, a slow and agonizing death by the Ricin poison, or you can embrace your true calling and return to the Soviet fold.'

Reinhardt resumed in Bavarian 'they were both not like you, Dan. one was too impulsive and foolish. The other a big head filled with emptiness. They had one job to stay low but they flaunt their discretion out to the public. Can you believe Day almost started a revolution in the university. The revolution is going to come but not in the hands of a careless happy fool like him.'

Reinhardt 'I admit Daniel. You're good. You left espionage and managed to lay so low you earned the trust of everyone and every system we tried so hard to perpetrate. Now I know you didn't do it deliberately. But kudos to you for not being found out. You were so good you even interviewed your brother and pretended the whole time you were not a part of them..;

'I'm not a part of you Reinhardt!' Daniel snapped and yelled at Reinhardt in German.

'Relax, relax...Dan. You don't want these English idiots things we are not getting along too well.' Reinhardt looked around everyone in the room with a cringe smile on his face.

'I don't want to have to kill you Dan. we are both old men. We can't keep playing kids game' Reinhardt continued in German.

‘C’mon man to man. Understand me. You just need to return and blend back in. now you know some of your superiors are as involved as we are, you know any wrong move means you get found out. You get found out and we’ll be tossing to your glass of Ricin poison.’

‘I mean, what you have to lose Daniel’ Reinhardt said in English.

Daniel's mind raced as he weighed his options. The grim reality of his situation hung heavy in the air. He knew that defying Reinhardt and Gilla would lead to his demise, and yet, surrendering to their demands meant embracing a life he had fought so hard to leave behind. It was a difficult choice, but Daniel couldn't bear the thought of leaving his fate in their hands.

With a deep breath, he looked directly into Reinhardt's eyes, his voice firm and resolute. "I'll resume my role. But, my life remains untouched. I'd rather take my own life than have you or Gilla do it for me."

Reinhardt's face contorted into a sinister grin, his eyes gleaming with satisfaction. "Ah, Daniel, always the dramatic one. Your death may be your choice, but make no mistake, you'll be bound by loyalty and secrecy until your last breath."

CHAPTER TWELVE

He found himself standing in a lush garden by the riverside, surrounded by vibrant flowers and towering trees. The air was filled with the sweet scent of blossoms, and the gentle breeze whispered melodies through the leaves.

The garden seemed to stretch infinitely in all directions, offering a tranquil sanctuary away from the chaos and troubles of the waking world. The colors were more vibrant, the scents more intoxicating, and the sounds more harmonious than anything he had ever experienced. The beauty of nature embraced him, filling his heart with a profound sense of peace and serenity.

As Daniel walked along the garden path, he marveled at the symphony of life that unfolded before him. Butterflies fluttered gracefully from one flower to another, their delicate wings painted in a myriad of iridescent hues. Birds perched on branches, their melodious songs echoing through the air. Bees buzzed busily from blossom to blossom, collecting nectar in their industrious dance.

The river flowed nearby, its crystal-clear waters meandering through the landscape like a silver ribbon. Daniel approached the riverbank and knelt down, dipping his fingers into the cool, refreshing water. He could feel its gentle caress, soothing his soul and washing away the worries that burdened him in the waking world.

In this ethereal realm, Daniel felt connected to the forces of nature in a way he had never experienced even on his way to the field of death. He closed his eyes and listened to the rustle of leaves, the whispers of the wind, and the gentle lapping of the river. He felt the warmth of the sun on his face, a tender kiss from the heavens above. It was as if he had become one with the garden, a part of this harmonious tapestry of life.

Time lost its meaning as Daniel wandered through the garden. He was a child again, exploring its hidden corners and secret pathways. He encountered cascading waterfalls that sparkled in the sunlight, their soothing rush of water a symphony of tranquility. He discovered hidden meadows blanketed in wildflowers, their vibrant colors painting the landscape like an artist's palette.

Amidst the beauty of this dream world, Daniel felt a deep sense of rejuvenation and renewal. The weight of his past burdens seemed to dissipate, replaced by a profound sense of liberation. Could be death he thought? The constraints of his earthly existence, had dissipated off his shoulders. He was free to immerse himself in the wonders of nature and the limitless possibilities of his own imagination.

Daniel found himself lying on the soft grass, gazing up at the clear blue sky above. He watched as fluffy white clouds drifted lazily by, their ever-changing shapes forming familiar faces and whimsical creatures. He giggled, feeling a childlike joy bubble up within him, untethered by the worries and responsibilities of adulthood.

He plucked a wildflower from the ground and held it in his hand, marveling at its delicate petals and intricate design. He closed his eyes and inhaled its fragrance, allowing its essence to infuse his senses with a profound sense of calm and contentment.

Suddenly he felt a pull. It started from his cramp back, down to his cramp swollen legs. He sigh and held on to his back hoping the pain would go away. But it didn't. It was time to return.

Daniel opened his eyes to the confines of the facility, deep within the bowels of British intelligence. The atmosphere within was cold and sterile, the air heavy with a sense of hollowness and isolation. The labyrinth of hallways, surveillance cameras, and reinforced steel doors, were his only companion in prison.

The room where Daniel was held captive was small and windowless, the only source of light emanating from a single dim overhead bulb. The walls were made of cold, gray concrete, giving the room a gloomy and oppressive feeling. The floor was bare, except for a worn-out rug that added a touch of discomfort to the already bleak surroundings.

The furniture in the room was minimalistic yet functional. There was a plain, metal-framed bed with a thin mattress that offered little comfort. A small table stood against one wall, accompanied by a solitary chair. The table held a few basic necessities—a water pitcher, a tea pot and cup, and a plate with meager food portions.

Cameras were strategically placed in every corner, monitoring Daniel's every move. Daniel sat up from his bed to look at them. His back pain and leg cramps intensified landing him solidly in the reality he currently was.

Time seemed to stretch endlessly in this sterile and isolated environment. Days blurred together, marked only by the routine visits from the interrogators. Their presence was intimidating, their expressions stern and impassive. They would enter the room, armed with a barrage of questions and accusations, probing deep into Daniel's past and present. Their interrogation tactics were designed to break his spirit, to extract every piece of information they believed he possessed.

As the days turned into weeks, Daniel's sense of isolation grew. There were no human interactions outside of the interrogations, leaving him to grapple with his own thoughts and doubts. The silence that filled the room was deafening, and the absence of any connection to the outside world weighed heavily on his psyche.

In this confined space, Daniel's mind became both his greatest companion and his fiercest enemy. Memories, regrets, and unanswered questions haunted him in the solitude of his confinement. He replayed his past actions, scrutinizing every decision he had made, searching for answers that seemed forever out of reach.

Within the confines of his cell, Daniel's mind wandered back to the events that led him to this moment. After he made the decision to return to the world of espionage after the shocking revelation of Graham and Gilla's betrayal.

He recalled the conversation with Reinhardt, where he was given the ultimatum to either succumb to the fate of the Ricin poison or resume his role as a Soviet spy. It was a choice between certain death or a life of deception and danger. In that moment, Daniel decision that moment was not based on his animalistic instincts to survive but his readiness to end thing once and for all. He had made up his mind he would not die till his death was worth it and so thing was an opening for him

Still as he replayed those memories in his mind, he couldn't help but feel a sense of guilt and regret. He had chosen to enter this treacherous world again, knowing the risks and the potential harm he could cause. But he also knew that he had a greater purpose—a mission to uncover the conspiracy that threatened the prime minister and the stability of his country.

In the days leading up to his capture, Daniel had painstakingly gathered evidence, piecing together the puzzle of the conspiracy that extended far beyond Reinhardt and Gilla. He had discovered the involvement of high-ranking officials, including Graham and many others, whom he once considered a trusted ally. The extent of the betrayal ran deep, and he knew that if he were to expose the truth, he would have to play his cards carefully and strategically.

The days turned into weeks, and Daniel's determination to uncover the truth only intensified. He used his advantage as a spy in the establishment meticulously plan his next moves, analyzing every detail and considering every possible outcome. He knew that his escape and the exposure of the conspiracy relied on his ability to outwit not only Reinhardt and Gilla but also the powerful individuals pulling the strings behind the scenes.

As Daniel's mind delved deeper into a way out, a realization struck him with profound force. It became clearer to him more and more that Mason, his former colleague and comrade, had been nothing more than a pawn in a much larger game—a game orchestrated by powers far beyond their reach.

He vividly recalled the time when their paths crossed, back in the days when their shared sense of duty bound them together. Mason had always been a steadfast and dedicated agent, driven by a genuine desire to protect their country. They had worked side by side, trusting one another implicitly.

Daniel realized that the high-profile press conference were Mason had been instructed to make false claims about Day, was a manipulation by forces higher than he was.

The pieces of the puzzle started to align, revealing a sinister game of manipulation and deceit. It became evident that there were forces at play, operating from the shadows, pulling strings and orchestrating events to serve their own agenda. Mason, unwittingly caught in the crossfire, had become a pawn in their grand scheme.

The plot to kill the prime minister and a member of the royal family was far from over. And Graham, whom he had once regarded as a trusted ally, had become the puppet master, safeguarding the sinister plan from the shadows.

Daniel recalled a pivotal moment in the battle against the plot to assassinate the prime minister. It was a time when Mason had mustered the courage to confront Graham, without the knowledge of him manning the orchestration of things. The scene unfolded in a dimly lit room, the air heavy with tension and the weight of hidden agendas.

Mason, resolute and unwavering, stood before a table covered with stacks of evidence, meticulously gathered to expose the truth. His eyes burned with determination as he passionately presented his findings, his voice resonating with conviction and a sense of duty. He laid bare the intricate connections and unveiled the nefarious plot that threatened the very fabric of their nation.

That was the first time in a long time that Daniel had seen Mason so bold and passionate about something that doesn't benefit him directly. It was a sight that boosted Daniel's belief in a way out.

But Graham, a master manipulator and skilled tactician, refused to yield to the truth. With a cold, calculated demeanor, he dismissed the evidence as mere fabrications, painting Mason as a misguided and delusional individual. Each word that left Graham's lips was laced with poison, twisting the narrative and turning the tables against the valiant efforts of his adversary.

Daniel as he witnessed this confrontation could feel a flame rising within him. It was perhaps a mix of anger and optimism. Seeing Mason remaining steadfast, refusing to be silenced was a sight he never thought he needed to see. His voice quivered with a mix of frustration and determination as he stood against Graham's passiveness in handling the assassination matter.

Graham's machinations, however, had devastating consequences. In a calculated move, he stripped Mason of his rank and authority, effectively cutting off his access to critical resources and support. The blow struck deep, leaving Mason surprised and wounded. Perhaps it was more of a startle than a surprise feeling Mason had that moment. He was shocked at Graham's capricious action. Something that was totally out of his character. But Graham had carefully orchestrated this to ensure his compliance and to extinguish any flicker of resistance.

Daniel watched in anguish as his comrade. Now that they both had a burning desire for retribution, he knew he found an ally. Daniel understood that he couldn't face the dangerous web of conspiracy alone. He needed allies. The plot to assassinate the prime minister continues and time was far from been on his side.

Although Mason had been implicated in the events, he believed that Mason was innocent, just like himself—a pawn in a much larger game. But convincing Mason to join forces wouldn't be easy.

Through covert channels and encrypted messages, Daniel reached out to Mason, urging him to meet in a secluded location. The meeting was fraught with tension and suspicion. Mason was understandably wary of Daniel's motives, unsure if he could trust anyone after everything that had transpired.

Daniel laid out the evidence he had gathered—the connections, the hidden agendas, the threads that tied Graham and the other conspirators to the plot to Mason. He spoke of the imminent danger that loomed over the prime minister and the royal family, emphasizing the need to act swiftly and decisively.

Mason had raised an eyebrow, an amused smirk playing at the corners of his lips. "Oh, Daniel, my friend," he chuckled. "You always had a flair for the dramatic. Are you telling me you've stumbled upon a grand conspiracy? Have you been watching too many spy movies lately?" Mason chuckled slightly and continued. ‘I’ve always known age only keeps getting harsher on you Daniel.’

Daniel knew that convincing Mason would be no easy task, but he never expected this form of debasement in the process.

"No, Mason," Daniel had said firmly. "This is not a fabrication or a figment of my imagination. Look..." he pointed at the piles of scattered files on the table.

Mason's laughter faded, replaced by a growing curiosity. His eyes flickered with a mixture of surprise and intrigue as he leaned forward, his SCEPTICISM momentarily pushed aside. "Show me," he urged, his voice now tinged with a newfound seriousness.

Daniel pushed a folder to Mason. He opened it slowly, revealing a meticulous collection of documents, photographs, and reports. Each piece of evidence was like a puzzle piece, fitting together to form a damning picture of corruption and manipulation.

As Mason flipped through the pages, his expression changed from mild interest to shock. The laughter that had danced on his lips vanished, replaced by a solemn gaze. The pieces of the puzzle were fitting together too perfectly, too convincingly for him to ignore.

"This shit runs longer than I ever imagined.' his eyes widen in shock 'How did you... how did you uncover all of this?'

The room fell into a heavy silence as Mason continued to peruse the evidence. The weight of the truth bore down on them both, the gravity of the situation sinking in with each passing moment. It was as if the walls of their reality were crumbling, revealing the sinister machinations that had remained hidden for far too long.

Finally, Mason looked up, his eyes meeting Daniel's with a newfound determination. "We can't ignore this, Daniel. We can't let this slide. These people, they've infiltrated the very institutions meant to protect us. We have a duty to expose them" on Mason’s face was the same determination and readiness he saw in Graham’s office. This filled Daniel up with more courage.

In the days that followed, Daniel and Mason regrouped, strategizing and plotting their next move. Since they could not rely on the established channels of power. They needed to find allies in unexpected places, individuals whose unwavering commitment to truth and justice could help expose the dark underbelly of the communist infiltrators.

Amealia was their first go to. She had long suspected that her late husband, Finnan, had been entangled in something dangerous. She had grown suspicious of his secretive activities and his sudden change in behaviour before his untimely demise. When Daniel and Mason approached her, she was hesitant but intrigued. They revealed the truth about the communist infiltrators and Finnan's unwitting involvement in the conspiracy.

Over a series of covert meetings, Daniel, Mason, and Amealia meticulously devised a plan to expose the evidence to the media and the public. They understood that they needed a significant platform to ensure that the revelations would have a lasting impact, and Amealia's connections in the media proved to be the perfect conduit.

Their first task was to compile and organize the evidence they had gathered. Daniel and Mason had meticulously documented the infiltrators, their connections, and their involvement in the plot to assassinate the prime minister and a member of the royal family. The information included financial records, encrypted messages, and testimonies from insiders who had seen the conspiracy unfold firsthand.

As they sifted through the evidence, Daniel, Mason, and Amealia created a comprehensive timeline that detailed the events leading up to the present moment. They aimed to present a clear and compelling narrative that would leave no doubt about the existence of the communist infiltration and the imminent danger facing the country's leadership.

Simultaneously, they worked on securing safe channels to release the evidence to the media. They reached out to trusted journalists and investigative reporters, carefully vetting their backgrounds and ensuring their dedication to uncovering the truth. They knew that their actions could potentially jeopardize their own safety, and they needed to be cautious in selecting reliable allies who shared their commitment to justice.

With the evidence compiled and the media connections in place, Daniel, Mason, and Amealia prepared for the critical moment—the full-blown reveal mission. They understood the importance of timing and coordination to maximize the impact of their revelations. They meticulously mapped out the sequence of events, ensuring that each step would unfold seamlessly.

The first step was to disseminate the evidence to the media. Daniel and Mason, accompanied by Amealia, met with the trusted journalists and handed over the meticulously organized files containing the incriminating evidence. They stressed the significance of the information and the urgent need to bring it to light. The journalists, fueled by the gravity of the situation, pledged to investigate thoroughly and prepare for the imminent media storm.

Next, they strategized the release of a comprehensive exposé. Mason, and Amealia decided to hold a press conference, where they would present a condensed version of the evidence and unveil the shocking truth to the world. The press conference would serve as a catalyst, ensuring that the media's attention would be firmly focused on the revelations.

They selected a secure location for the press conference—a place where they could control access and minimize the risk of interference. Mason enlisted the help of a trusted team to handle logistics and security, ensuring that their mission would not be compromised.

As the day of the press conference arrived, and anticipation filled the air. Mason, and Amealia took their places behind the podium, ready to unveil the truth. The room was packed with journalists, cameras, and recording devices—a testament to the magnitude of the impending revelations. Mason believed this to a moment to right the wrongs he had been manipulated to perform. While Amealia saw this as a full blown revenge mission. The people who killed her husbands had no right to infiltrate the nation she loves so much.

For Daniel this was a difficult decision. He had made the difficult decision to succumb to Reinhardt's pressure in order to protect those he cared about, but he also knew that this compromise could potentially tarnish his reputation and implicate him in the very plot he was trying to dismantle.

However, the urgency of the situation left no time for hesitation or second thoughts. The clock was ticking, and the threat to the prime minister's life loomed closer with each passing moment. Daniel understood that sacrificing his own reputation was a small price to pay in comparison to the countless lives at stake. This was him giving back what he had held so dearly and greedily all his life; his life.

Taking a deep breath, Mason addressed the gathered audience of journalists and reporters. He began by revealing the extent of the communist infiltration within the police and military, emphasizing the imminent danger that the prime minister and the royal family faced. He explained the intricate web of deceit, naming key players and presenting the evidence they had meticulously gathered.

As Mason spoke, he could feel the weight of his own culpability bearing down upon him. He knew that his admission of involvement in the conspiracy would have repercussions, but he also recognized that his actions were driven by a genuine desire to protect his country and its leaders.

The room fell into a stunned silence as Mason's words reverberated through the air. Journalists frantically scribbled notes, capturing every detail of his revelations. Cameras clicked and whirred, recording the gravity of the moment. It was a turning point—an exposé that would shake the very foundations of British society.

Daniel, as he sat at the rear end of the press conference, knew that the consequences of his actions would unfold in the aftermath of the press conference. The fallout would be unpredictable, and he braced himself for the inevitable storm that would follow. He hoped that these revelations would shed light on the larger conspiracy, forcing the public in pressure who those needed to be pressured and sparked the movement to dismantle the communist infiltrators once and for all.

As the press conference came to a close, Mason and Amealia left the podium, their hearts heavy with a mix of relief and uncertainty. They had taken a monumental step in exposing the truth, but they were acutely aware of the challenges that lay ahead. The fallout from their revelations would be swift and potentially devastating, as the forces of power and influence fought back to protect their secrets.

In the days that followed, the media frenzy surrounding the exposé intensified. The evidence presented by Daniel and Mason was scrutinized and debated, and the public's reaction varied. Some applauded their courage in unveiling the truth, while others questioned their motives and expressed SCEPTICISM. The political landscape shifted, as politicians and public figures were forced to respond to the revelations and take a stance against the infiltrators.

Daniel vividly remembered the morning when the newspaper publication hit the stands. The front page featured bold headlines, exposing the communist infiltration within the police and military and detailing the plot to assassinate the prime minister and a member of the royal family. The revelations sent shockwaves through the nation, and the public was left reeling with a mixture of disbelief, anger, and fear.

As the news spread like wildfire, the authorities scrambled to respond. Arrest warrants were swiftly issued for the key individuals implicated in the conspiracy, including high-ranking officials, police officers, and military personnel. The arrests were made with a sense of urgency, as the threat of the impending assassinations still loomed large.

The public's trust in the security apparatus had been shattered, and confidence needed to be restored. The authorities initiated a thorough investigation, temporarily confining several individuals for questioning to ascertain the extent of their involvement and gather additional evidence. The confinements were seen as a necessary step to ensure the safety of the public and prevent any potential retaliation or further attempts to destabilize the country.

Mason, Amealia and Daniel were arrested. This was called a temporary confinement by the authorities.

However, Daniel in his confinement knew that this was just the beginning of a long and arduous process to uproot the communist infiltrators and rebuild the integrity of the institutions they had compromised. It was a delicate balance between ensuring justice and preserving the rights of those who might have been unwitting pawns in the conspiracy.

The temporary confinements sparked public debates and discussions. Some viewed them as necessary precautions to ensure the thorough investigation of all individuals involved, while others raised concerns about potential abuses of power and the presumption of innocence. The media played a crucial role in holding the authorities accountable, scrutinizing the process and providing updates on the ongoing investigations.

In the midst of the chaos, Daniel continued to play his part, providing additional information and cooperating with the authorities. He knew that his own involvement in the conspiracy would be examined closely, but he remained steadfast in his commitment to bringing the truth to light and ensuring that those responsible faced the consequences of their actions.

As the investigations progressed, more pieces of the puzzle fell into place. The evidence gathered by Daniel, Mason, and their allies proved instrumental in identifying the extent of the communist infiltration and unearthing the intricate network of conspirators. The temporary confinements yielded valuable information, allowing the authorities to connect the dots and dismantle the remaining elements of the plot.

In the days and weeks that followed, the confinements gradually came to an end. Mason, Amealia, and some other individuals were cleared of any involvement, while others were formally charged and brought to trial. The legal process moved forward, with the accused facing the weight of the evidence against them. The nation watched as the justice system sought to hold the perpetrators accountable for their actions and restore a sense of trust and security.

As the investigations into the communist plot unfolded, the authorities made significant progress. Graham, one of the key players safeguarding the conspiracy in the shadows, was finally apprehended. His arrest marked a crucial step towards dismantling the network of infiltrators and holding them accountable for their actions.

However, Reinhardt managed to evade capture, slipping through the authorities' grasp. His escape only added to the urgency of bringing him to justice, as he remained a significant threat to national security and the lives of high-ranking officials.

Meanwhile, Gilla, another individual implicated in the conspiracy, was not as fortunate as Reinhardt. She was apprehended. The authorities recognized the value of her testimony and the potential information she held. Daniel recalled the day she was arrested. He stood hidden among the bustling crowd of security and British intelligence, his gaze fixed on the commotion that surrounded Gilla.

His eyes locked with Gilla's, but her once warm and vibrant gaze now appeared cold and distant. There was a silent exchange between them, an unspoken understanding that their paths had diverged irreversibly.

Gilla stood tall, her poise unyielding despite the circumstances. Her hands were firmly clasped behind her back, the cold metal of handcuffs biting into her wrists. The police officers surrounding her were stern and unwavering.

Daniel couldn't bring himself to tear his gaze away from Gilla, his mind flooded with memories of their shared past. He recalled the moments they had spent together, their laughter and whispered confidences. They had been comrades in a battle against corruption, united by a common cause.

As the officers escorted Gilla away, a hush fell over the crowd. The world seemed to stand still for a moment, as if acknowledging the gravity of the situation. Daniel's heart ached, knowing that he might never see her again, that this moment could be their final goodbye.

Gilla's eyes bore into Daniel's, filled with a myriad of emotions. There was a silent plea, a yearning for him to understand the depths of the betrayal and the sacrifices she had made. But there was also a painful resignation, a knowledge that their paths had diverged and their fates were now inextricably tied to different destinies.

Daniel found it strange how he felt that moment. Despite what she had done, He wanted to reach out, to comfort her, to tell her that everything would be alright. But he remained rooted to the spot, unsure of how to make sense of the way he felt that moment.

As the police officers led Gilla away, Daniel watched her recede into the distance, swallowed by the harsh reality of her circumstances. The world around him resumed its frenetic pace, but Daniel felt as if time had stood still. His heart ached with a deep sense of loss, an ache that would linger long after Gilla's figure disappeared from view. Maybe Mason was right, perhaps he was getting senile

Mason, despite his involvement in the investigation and his efforts to expose the truth, found himself summoned for multiple thorough questioning. The authorities, seeking to fully comprehend the depth of his involvement and verify the veracity of his claims, subjected him to intense scrutiny. Mason cooperated fully, providing additional information and corroborating evidence to support the ongoing investigation.

After a thorough examination, the authorities concluded that Mason's involvement had been unwitting. His cooperation, along with the evidence presented, convinced them of his innocence. Consequently, he was released, relieved to have been exonerated from any direct involvement in the conspiracy.

Daniel, on the other hand, faced a different fate. His involvement in espionage ran deeper than. Despite Mason's fervent efforts to prove his innocence, the weight of his past espionage activities was used against him. The British intelligence, in their investigation, had uncovered Daniel's deep records in espionage, revealing a complicated history that cast doubt on his motives and allegiances.

The revelations of Daniel's past espionage activities shook the public's perception of him. The media, always hungry for sensational stories, latched onto the information, further tarnishing his reputation. Accusations of double-crossing and betrayals began to circulate, clouding the true intentions behind Daniel's recent actions.

The British intelligence, armed with the knowledge of Daniel's past, used it as a basis for his arrest. They saw him as a potential risk, a man with a complex history and connections that could compromise ongoing operations. Despite Mason's relentless efforts to advocate for Daniel's innocence and highlight his dedication to uncovering the truth, the evidence presented was deemed substantial enough to justify his arrest.

Daniel found himself confined once again, this time under the watchful eye of the British intelligence. Cut off from the outside world, he had to confront the consequences of his actions and the weight of his past.

The public's perception of Daniel's arrest varied. Some believed that his past indiscretions and involvement in espionage made him a liability, while others saw it as a calculated move by those who sought to suppress the truth. The media continued to speculate, dissecting every detail of his case and questioning the motives behind his actions.

As Daniel's mind wandered in his confinement, his thoughts turned to Gilla. In the days and weeks that followed, Daniel grappled with the haunting image of Gilla's arrest. He replayed the scene in his mind, dissecting every detail, searching for answers that seemed elusive. Was Gilla also a pawn in the game? What had led Gilla to this point, where silence and distance were her only response? The answers eluded him, buried deep within the labyrinth of betrayal and deception.

The prison walls stood tall and imposing, casting a gloomy shadow over Daniel's world. Days turned into weeks, weeks into months, and the isolation had taken its toll. The monotony of his existence was broken only by the occasional interactions with the guards or the fleeting glimpses of a few other inmates and the multiple characters in his lucid dreaming. Visitors were a rare occurrence, and Daniel had long resigned himself to the idea that he was destined to face his sentence alone.

But that day, as the heavy iron door swung open, a wave of surprise washed over Daniel. Standing in the doorway was Mason, his familiar face etched with a mix of concern and determination. It had been months since Daniel had seen a long familiar face, and he was taken aback by Mason's unexpected presence.

Daniel remained silent, his eyes fixed on Mason's face. He observed him with the gaze of someone who had been deprived of human connection for far too long. His senses heightened, attuned to every nuance, every flicker of emotion that passed across Mason's features.

Mason took a step forward, cautiously entering the small, confined space that served as a meeting room. The door closed behind him, sealing them off from the outside world. There was a weary awkwardness in the air. One that Daniel and Mason could not escape.

"Daniel," Mason sighed, his voice filled with a soberness. "I'm sorry it took so long to come and visit. I should have been here sooner."

Daniel's silence persisted, he needed to be sure he had not slide into another lucid dreaming again. He needed to sure it was really Mason there. Mason always started his conversation with his quirky sense of humor. Perhaps this was another character.

Mason moved closer to Daniel. ‘Yea, you look like shit.’ he said and gave a warm smile. It’s Mason, Daniel thought and sat up to look at him very well.

Mason didn't respond to his joke and sighed again. 'I know that things have been difficult for you. I can't even begin to imagine what you've been through.'

A flicker of emotion passed through Daniel's eyes, a glimmer of hope amidst the despair. Mason saw that and smiled. 'Yea, you're fine.'

The room seemed to come alive as Mason spoke, the walls closing in as their shared determination filled the air. Mason found a small stool and sat close to Daniel's cell as he talked about the recent occurrences that had happened while he's away. Daniel was not sure which he enjoyed. Mason's precise report about everything he wanted to hear and everything he did or Mason's flat quirky sense of humor that accompany every news and his gee as he told them

‘So, I got a promotion." He paused smiling, ‘...Officer of Duty, taking over Graham's position."

Daniel's eyes widened ever so slightly, a flicker of surprise breaking through his stoic facade. That’s rich coming from someone who will pick a pot of tea before duty.

Mason continued, his voice filled with a newfound determination. "With this promotion, I will have more access, more influence within the system. I intend to use every resource at my disposal to clear the infiltrators totally out of the system and to ensure that your case is heard and that the truth prevails."

Daniel bowed his head and sigh. The last time Mason was there which was probably several month now. He had said the same thing. Only that time he was not the

Officer of Duty. Daniel wasn't holding his breath on that. He believe this is the place he will die. Still he knew how tenacious Mason could be when be when he wants something done.

Mason continued with how the exciting the press and media attention he had gotten due to his exposure of the infiltrators was. The media had crowned him a hero of Great Britain and the queen was considering knighting him.

Daniel's imagined Mason standing as the center of attention, surrounded by a throng of reporters and journalists. Mason appeared confident, his posture exuding a self-assuredness that Daniel had not seen in him before. His voice carried through the air, captivating the eager ears that hung on his every word. The press, hungry for a story, bombarded him with questions, flashing their cameras and recording devices in his face.

Mason reveled in the spotlight, his smile widening as he fielded questions and offered carefully crafted responses. The reporters hung onto his every word, their pens scribbling furiously across notepads, eager to capture the essence of his newfound success.

As he imagined, his emotions tangled in a web of conflicting feelings. On one hand, he couldn't help but feel a sense of pride for his friend. Mason's unwavering dedication and tireless efforts had not gone unnoticed. He had fought tooth and nail to shed light on the injustices that had plagued Daniel's life.

Yet, beneath the pride, there was a twinge of bitterness. Daniel couldn't help but feel a little pang of jealousy, that could have been him. It was a bitter reminder of his own confinement, his voice silenced and his presence forgotten by the outside world.

Daniels mind shifted back to Mason speaking. Mason spoke of the time he was invited by the queen to Buckingham palace. As Mason spoke, Daniel made his mind travelled, imagining every detail of Mason's word alongside his imagination of things.

The grand hall of Buckingham Palace shimmering under the soft glow of chandeliers. Its opulent decorations a testament to the history and grandeur of the British monarchy. The evening was alive with the melodies of an orchestra, the mingling of esteemed guests, and the air of anticipation that comes with such prestigious events.

Mason stood among the sea of elegantly dressed individuals, his heart pounding with nervous excitement. This was a rare opportunity, an evening orchestrated by the Queen herself, and he intended to make the most of it. With each passing moment, he scanned the room, searching for a glimpse of the man whose attention he sought—the Prime Minister.

As the evening progressed, Mason's anticipation grew. He had spent countless hours preparing for this moment, rehearsing the words he would speak, the plea he would make on behalf of his friend Daniel. It was a daunting task, but one he had committed himself to, driven by the unwavering belief in Daniel's innocence and the debt he owed him.

Finally, he spotted him—a tall figure clad in a tailored suit, his presence commanding the attention of those around him. The

Prime Minister moved with ease through the crowd, engaging in animated conversations with influential individuals. Mason's heart skipped a beat as he realized this was his chance, the moment he had been waiting for.

Mason maneuvered through the crowd, his steps purposeful and focused. He weaved past socialites and diplomats, his sights firmly fixed on his target. Every passing second brought him closer to the Prime Minister, the weight of Daniel's fate heavy on his shoulders.

As Mason closed the gap, he could feel the adrenaline coursing through his veins. "Prime Minister," he called out, his voice echoing against the grandeur of the palace walls. The words hung in the air, momentarily capturing the attention of those nearby. The Prime Minister turned, his expression a mix of surprise and curiosity.

He had to make this encounter count, to seize the opportunity and make the Prime Minister understand the gravity of Daniel's situation. With a final burst of energy, Mason reached the Prime Minister's side, breathless but resolved.

Mason pushed forward without any self-consciousness, his voice steady as he began to recount the tale that had brought them together. "Sir, I must speak to you about a man named Daniel Carter. He is wrongly imprisoned, and his life has been unjustly taken away."

The Prime Minister regarded Mason with a mixture of interest and SCEPTICISM. "And who, may I ask, are you to make such claims?" he inquired, his tone laced with polite SCEPTICISM.

Mason took a deep breath, summoning every ounce of courage within him. "Sir, I am Mason. The new Office in the duty appointed by the cabinet in place of Graham Harlod. Daniel saved your life, risking his own to protect you. He is innocent, wrongly accused and convicted. I implore you, please look into his case. Consider the evidence, the injustices he has suffered. He deserves a fair trial, a chance at justice!"

As the words left Mason's lips, he watched the Prime Minister closely, searching for any flicker of understanding, any indication that his pleas were being heard. The seconds stretched into what felt like an eternity, the weight of his words hanging in the air.

Finally, the Prime Minister's expression softened, a glimmer of empathy breaking through his stoic facade. "Mason, is it? Your brilliant suit got me distracted. I'm aware of what you did for me and the nation." he said, his voice carrying a touch of sincerity. "I appreciate your passion and conviction. I assure you, I will personally look into this matter. No one should be denied justice."

Relief washed over Mason, his heart soaring with a renewed sense of hope. To have the Prime Minister's assurance, his promise to investigate Daniel's case, was more than he could have hoped for in that moment. Daniel's imagination shut on him that moment like a closed door bring him back to the cold hollow cell he currently was.

In the face of Daniel's prolonged silence, doubts began to cloud Mason's mind. Had Daniel gone round the bend? Had his efforts been in vain?

The air inside the prison cell grew heavy with anticipation as Mason, determined to break through Daniel's silence, clutched onto the letter from Gilla. He knew that this piece of correspondence held the potential to ignite a spark within his friend, to finally pierce through the veil of detachment that had enveloped Daniel for far too long.

'Daniel.' he said and took out a letter from his pocket. "This is a letter from Gilla. It arrived a few days ago, and I thought it might help..."

'Gilla?' Daniel finally said. He was not sure if he had mouth it quietly or out loud but Mason's eyes brightened as he spoke. Daniel stretched his hands out the cell bar and collected the letter from Mason. He lifted it up in the air as if to see if it was really her. Quietly, he opened it and read its content.

The letter offered a glimpse into Gilla's past, shedding light on the circumstances that led her to become involved in espionage for the Soviet Union.

The letter spoke of Gilla's upbringing on a farm in rural France. She described a childhood marked by hardship and uncertainty, shaped by the shadow of her father's involvement with a fascist family. Gilla's father had fought for their cause, believing in their ideology, but he perished in the battle, leaving his family to bear the burden of his legacy.

Daniel made his mind wonder that moment to the picturesque countryside of rural France, nestled among rolling hills and fields of vibrant wildflowers. The quaint farmstead that stood in this frame.

Time seemed to stand still, and nature wrapped around every corner and the laughter of children echoed through the air. And in this idyllic setting was Gilla, a young girl who discovered the beauty of the world and the joy of innocent play.

Gilla, with her unruly golden curls and sparkling blue eyes, radiated an infectious energy that drew others to her. She was a free spirit, always in search of adventure and new discoveries. With the farm as her playground, she reveled in the simple pleasures that nature bestowed upon her.

In the early morning hours, as the first rays of sunlight kissed the dew-covered grass, Gilla would venture out into the meadows. The scent of wildflowers mingled with the crisp country air, filling her senses with a symphony of fragrances. She would tiptoe through the delicate blooms, her small hands gently brushing against their petals, as if in greeting.

The meadows became her canvas, and she painted with the colors of nature. With a handful of vibrant daisies and buttercups, she fashioned intricate floral crowns, adorning her head with a joyful abandon. The gentle breeze teased her hair, carrying whispers of secrets shared among the flowers.

The rivers that meandered through the farmland held a special allure for young Gilla. She would dip her bare feet into the cool, crystal-clear waters, giggling as the ripples tickled her skin. Her laughter mingled with the symphony of chirping birds and buzzing insects, creating a symphony of nature's orchestra.

Together with her childhood friends, the children of neighboring farmers, Gilla would embark on grand adventures. They would explore the woods that bordered their homes, forging paths through the dense underbrush, their imaginations transforming the forest into a realm of untold wonders.

In the shade of towering oak trees, Gilla and her friends would build makeshift shelters, fashioning homes out of fallen branches and moss-covered stones. With mud-streaked faces and hands, they would play games of make-believe, their imaginations transporting them to faraway lands and heroic quests.

The farm animals, too, were an integral part of Gilla's friend group. She would spend hours in the company of gentle cows, their warm breaths brushing against her cheek as she whispered secrets in their ears. The goats would frolic around her, their playful antics drawing peals of laughter from the depths of her being. And the chickens, with their vibrant plumage, would follow her like a colorful entourage, clucking and pecking at the ground as they went.

As the sun would dip below the horizon, casting a warm golden glow over the countryside, Gilla and her friends would gather around a crackling bonfire. They would share stories and dreams, their youthful voices carrying on the breeze, mingling with the chorus of crickets. They would marvel at the twinkling stars above, imagining the countless possibilities that awaited them.

In those innocent moments, surrounded by the beauty of the natural world, Gilla was happy. The simplicity of life on the farm, the connection to the earth and its creatures, instilled in her a deep appreciation for the wonders that lay all around.

As World War II raged on, the peaceful and idyllic life that Gilla had known on the rural farm in France was abruptly shattered. The arrival of the Nazis brought fear, chaos, and an immense darkness that enveloped the once serene landscapes. The contrast between the picturesque nature life she had cherished and the harsh realities of war was stark, casting a long shadow over her innocent existence.

Gilla witnessed the transformation of her surroundings with a heavy heart. The meadows that once bloomed with wildflowers were now trampled under the boots of soldiers. The streams that once gurgled with laughter were tainted with the echoes of gunshots and the cries of anguish. The world she had known, where children played freely and the beauty of nature danced in harmony, was replaced by an atmosphere of mistrust, secrecy, and betrayal.

Amidst the chaos, Gilla's father, once a pillar of strength and love in her life, changed. The occupation had twisted his values and manipulated his loyalties. The fear and pressure exerted by the Nazi regime had eroded his moral compass, turning him into a willing informant. Gilla watched in horror as he snitched on a Jewish family. They were dragged out of their hiding place like rodents, all nine of them and mocked by the Nazi soldiers who made a spot of them and made them perform nasty acts to their entertainment. Clarie, her childhood friend was amidst this family. She had cried and cried till her face turned bright red like it would pop any moment. The Nazi soldiers where bored, the shot every one of them on the head. Clarie was the last one. The solder who was to shoot her slipped a little as he target her and the bullet flied off to her temples tearing of a side of her head. She had landed on the floor, crawling off in agony as her head gush blood into the bright green of the field. She screamed in agony as she fought for her life crawling of the fire like a snail racing off to escape its captors' grip of its shell. The solder finally ended her pain with a bullet at the back of her skull.

It was a pivotal moment that shattered Gilla's innocence and forever altered her perception of the world. The image of the Jewish family, their faces etched with fear and despair, haunted her dreams. She was consumed by a deep sense of guilt, knowing that she had been a witness to their betrayal, powerless to intervene or save them from their tragic fate.

Gilla in the letter continued, as she recounted the struggles her family faced, ostracized and shunned by the community due to their association with fascism. Determined to clear her family's name and find a sense of purpose, Gilla was drawn into the world of espionage. The Soviet Union, recognizing her potential and her desire for redemption, recruited her as a covert operative.

In her letter, Gilla expressed the conflicted emotions that plagued her throughout her espionage career. She revealed the weight of her past and the constant internal struggle between loyalty to her family's memory and the cause she had been thrust into. Gilla's motivations were complex, driven by a desire to prove herself, seek justice, and protect the vulnerable from the oppression she had witnessed.

Daniel, as he read the letter, began to understand the depth of Gilla's involvement in the conspiracy. His answers presented to him in plain sight. Her past, intertwined with personal tragedy and a search for redemption, shed light on the complexities of her character. He realized that Gilla, unlike himself, had been shaped by circumstances beyond her control, forced into a life of secrecy and subterfuge.

As Daniel finished reading Gilla's letter, his heart sank with a mix of empathy and sorrow. The letter had offered a glimpse into her troubled past and the complexities that had driven her to become entangled in the web of espionage. The weight of her struggles and the choices she had made became all too real.

Just as Daniel was grappling with the implications of Gilla's story, Mason's expression became somber. 'She had asked me to give this to you yesterday evening. She was found dead in her cell this morning. Killed by Ricin again.'

This time involuntarily, Daniel's mind wandered to Gilla in her cell. She laying lifeless on the floor. Her organs paralyzed. Her gradual detachment from the world begins, as she feels her presence slowly dissolving. A sense of weightlessness may permeate the body, as if the constraints of gravity are loosening their grip. There may be a deep fatigue, as though the body, weary from its struggles, is yearning for rest.

The pain she feels subdued, replaced by a gentle numbing and a sensation akin to a distant echo. She hears a distant whisper, barely discernible amidst the tapestry of other sensations. Warmth through her veins, like the embrace of a comforting fire on a chilly evening.

Myriad of emotions to arise in her, ranging from tranquility and acceptance to fear and longing. Memories flushed in her mind, playing out montage of cherished moments, regrets, and unfinished dreams. The boundaries between her past, present, and future may blur, giving rise to a sense of timelessness.

The boundaries of self dissolve, and a profound sense of unity with the universe is experienced, likened to a merging with the cosmic fabric, an expansion of consciousness beyond the confines of her physical form. Time stands still, and a profound peace may envelop the dying, offering solace amidst the uncertainty.

When her journey nears its end, a sense of detachment from her physical body become more pronounced. The world fades, like a misty veil being drawn across a forgotten landscape. The fading bring forth a subtle detachment from the physical realm, as if the dying are gently unravelling from her earthly bonds. Her focus shifting inward, and the external world retreats to the periphery.

A deep sense of loss washed over Daniel. He mourned the loss of Gilla quietly. Mason understood he needed space left after the longest moment of silence he could endure. Daniel kept his grip on the letter, unable to cry though he felt a hurricane of emotions within him.

He managed to pull himself out of the thin laid bed and got up. Daniel, now an old man, his once vibrant and youthful features had weathered the passage of time, etching the stories of his experiences onto his face. Each wrinkle, every line, and the hint of grey in his hair spoke volumes of the hardships he had endured and the burdens he had carried.

His face, once chiseled and strong, now displayed the gentle weariness of age. Deep lines etched around his eyes, a testament to a lifetime of intense concentration and the strain of constantly assessing threats and risks. His eyes retained a glimmer of their former sharpness, hinting at the intelligence and resilience that lay within.

As Daniel's gaze wandered, his eyes conveyed a mix of wisdom and sadness. They held the weight of countless secrets, the memories of friends lost and missions unaccomplished. In their depths, one could glimpse the traces of a man who had seen both the best and worst of humanity.

His once firm jawline had softened, now carrying a hint of vulnerability and a touch of weariness. The years of facing adversity had taken their toll, leaving behind a quiet resolve tempered by the passage of time. Yet, within that ageing jawline, there still resided a trace of the strength and determination that had propelled him through countless trials.

Though his body had grown frail, there remained a quiet grace in his movements. Each step was measured and deliberate, a testament to a lifetime of discipline and training. Through the years had slowed his pace.

Daniel's hands were weathered and lined with age spots. They had once been the tools of his trade—swift, agile, and capable of both destruction and creation. Now, they carried the marks of time, the proof of a life spent navigating danger and embracing the weight of responsibility.

As his fingers gently traced the contours of his face, the texture of his skin revealed the passage of time. It had lost some of its elasticity. His silver hair, thinning and wispy, framed his face with a quiet elegance. Each strand spoke of a lifetime of experiences, of hardships and triumphs, and the wisdom that can only come with the passage of time. Despite the thinning locks, his hair carried a distinguished air, a reminder of the years spent navigating the murky world of espionage.

Daniel finally stood up, his statue had diminished over the years, his once proud figure now slightly stooped. The weight of his experiences seemed to press upon his shoulders, as if reminding him of the countless burdens he had carried throughout his life.

He turned to gaze at the mirror on the wall of his cell. As Daniel gazed into the mirror, he sort tears but didn't find it. He wondered how tears had eluded him just like death had. His heart broken quietly within him and his voice echoes 'Gilla...' within his cell.

CHAPTER THIRTEEN

It was a new day, as Daniel stepped out to the glorious light of the day. Feeling a sense of anticipation in the air. The warm rays of sunshine enveloped him, casting a golden glow on the world around him. The sky was a pristine blue canvas, adorned with fluffy white clouds that seemed to dance with joy.

Taking a deep breath, Daniel felt the freshness of the air filling his lungs. It was as if every inhalation brought with it a sense of freedom and renewed energy. The scent of blooming flowers wafted through the gentle breeze, carrying with it the promise of new beginnings.

As he walked along the familiar path, Daniel couldn't help but notice the vibrant colors that painted the landscape. The lush green grass beneath his feet seemed to come alive, swaying gently as if it were greeting him. The trees stood tall and proud, their leaves rustling in harmony with the wind, creating a soothing melody.

Birds chirped cheerfully, their melodious songs filling the air with a symphony of nature's music. Daniel paused to watch as they soared through the sky, their wings gliding effortlessly against the backdrop of the endless horizon. It was a sight that reminded him of the boundless possibilities that life held.

The world around him seemed to come alive, vibrant and teeming with life. Bees buzzed from flower to flower, diligently collecting nectar. Butterflies gracefully fluttered in the air, their delicate wings a kaleidoscope of colors. It was a testament to the intricate beauty and interconnectedness of the natural world.

Daniel found himself drawn to a nearby river, its crystal-clear waters glistening under the sunlight. He stood by its banks, mesmerized by the gentle ripples that cascaded across its surface. The tranquil sounds of the water flowing created a soothing backdrop, transporting him to a place of serenity and peace.

As he closed his eyes, Daniel could feel the warmth of the sun caressing his skin, infusing him with a sense of calm and contentment. It was a moment of pure bliss, a respite from the worries and complexities of life. In that tranquil oasis, he found solace and a renewed appreciation for the simple joys that nature offered.

Time seemed to stand still as Daniel allowed himself to be fully present in the moment. He embraced the beauty around him. This was his lucid dream come true. The symphony of sights, sounds, and sensations that enveloped him. It was a reminder that amidst the chaos and challenges of life, there was still immense beauty to be found.

He made his way to a nearby park and sat on a weathered wooden bench in the park, his gaze fixed on a group of children playing nearby. Their laughter filled the air, carrying with it a sense of unadulterated joy and boundless energy. It was a scene that warmed his heart and brought a gentle smile to his lips.

The children moved with an effortless grace, their small figures darting across the green grass like beams of sunlight. They chased each other in playful abandon, their laughter echoing through the trees. Their innocence was evident in every giggle, every wide-eyed expression that radiated pure delight.

Daniel watched as they played simple games, unaffected by the complexities of the world that lay beyond their youthful haven. Their imaginations knew no bounds as they transformed the park into a vast kingdom, where every tree became a castle and every flower a magical portal to another realm. Their unburdened spirits soared, untouched by the weight of responsibilities and worries that would inevitably come with age.

He observed their interactions, the way they shared toys and took turns with unwavering fairness. There was no room for prejudice or judgement in their innocent world. They embraced one another as friends, unconditionally accepting each other's quirks and idiosyncrasies. It was a lesson in human connection that transcended age, reminding Daniel of the simplicity and beauty of genuine companionship.

As he watched, memories of his own childhood flooded back, like fragments of a distant dream. He recalled the endless summer days spent in the neighborhood park, where time seemed to stretch infinitely. The innocence of youth had shielded him from the harsh realities of the world, allowing him to revel in the simple pleasures of play and exploration.

The children's laughter brought him back to the present, and he marveled at their ability to find joy in the smallest of things. They chased after bubbles that floated on the breeze, their eyes sparkling with wonder. Their laughter rang out like delicate bells, a melodic symphony that celebrated the beauty of the moment.

Daniel found himself captivated by their carefree spirits, envying their ability to live fully in the present. He longed for a return to that time of untainted innocence, when the world was a vast playground brimming with endless possibilities.

One little girl caught his attention. She had paused by a patch of wildflowers, her eyes wide with wonder as she admired the delicate petals swaying in the breeze. With a gentle touch, she plucked a daisy from the ground, her face illuminated with a radiant smile.

As the children continued their games, their laughter echoing through the park, Daniel felt a deep sense of gratitude. He realized that in witnessing their innocence, he was granted a glimpse into the purest aspects of humanity.

Two gentlemen who seem to be the fathers of the little children settled on the bench where Daniel was. One had a newspaper in his hands and they were both arguing vehemently about something. They both nodded at Daniel and continued.

They had contrasting demeanors—one tall and imposing with a stern expression, while the other was shorter and wore a contemplative look. He tall one wore a blue check t-shirt and a jean trousers while the shorter one wore a grey oversize suit.

Daniel couldn't help but overhear snippets of their conversation. The words "iron curtain" and "Soviet Union" hung in the air, immediately piquing his interest. He instinctively knew that their debate delve into the profound changes occurring in

Europe and the world while he had been in confinement.

The taller man, with a commanding presence, spoke first. His voice carried an air of certainty and authority. "The fall of the Iron Curtain was a necessary step towards freedom and progress. The Soviet Union's grip on Eastern Europe stifled individual liberties and economic growth. Its collapse signaled the triumph of democracy and the emergence of a new era."

The shorter man, who held on to the newspaper vehement, listened impatiently, waiting to offer his counterpoint. His face etched with lines of contemplation and irritation, "But we cannot not overlook the consequences of the Soviet Union's demise. The abrupt end of a superpower has unleashed a wave of economic and social upheaval. The transition to capitalism has left many struggling, with widening income disparities and lost livelihoods."

Their opposing viewpoints ignited a passionate exchange, with each man drawing on historical events and geopolitical dynamics to support their arguments.

"The fall of the Soviet Union allowed for the reunification of divided nations. It shattered the chains that had held Eastern Europe captive for decades. Countries once under Soviet control could now chart their own destinies, embrace democratic values, and forge alliances with the West. It paved the way for an era of greater global cooperation." the tall one said.

"You're not looking at the consequences Peter. The abrupt transition to capitalism left many ill-prepared for the shift. Look...'

he pointed at the newspaper in his hands. 'It has resulted in economic instability and social dislocation. See here..."The dismantling of state-run industries led to mass unemployment and economic inequality. We must acknowledge that progress often comes at a cost."' he read

As their arguments continued, Daniel found himself drawn into the conversation, he couldn't make sense of it at first. But he found himself drawn to Peter's optimism and the belief in the transformative power of democracy.

Yet, Alex's concerns brought a lot of questions to his mind. The sudden shift in economic systems? The fall of the Iron curtain? What was he talking about?

The scale of their dialogue got broader and broader. They talked about the future of Europe, the balance of power on the global stage, and the need for continued collaboration in the face of new challenges. It was an interesting clash of perspectives that mirrored the complexities of a changing world that Daniel had not gotten the chance to experience.

They delved into the future of Europe, their words became more animated, interlaced with a hint of a transition from the heated back and forth to a good-natured banter.

Peter leaned forward, a glimmer of excitement in his eyes. "The fall of the Iron Curtain opened up new possibilities for Europe though. With the barriers dissolved, we can expect a wave of integration and cooperation among nations. The European Union will flourish Alex! With such unity we get economic prosperity, cultural exchange, the shared commitment to democratic values and we can’t rule out the power that come with unity. It's a new era of unity and collective strength." he counted his hands as he listed his point

Alex chuckled softly, shaking his head. "Ah, Peter, always the optimist. While I appreciate your enthusiasm, let's not forget the inherent challenges of such a grand vision. The diverse histories, cultures, and economic systems within Europe will inevitably lead to tensions and disagreements. The path to unity will be riddled with obstacles."

Peter smiled back, undeterred by Alex's SCEPTICISM. "Of course, there will be hurdles along the way. But isn't that what makes it all the more exciting? Europe has weathered countless storms throughout its history, and it has emerged stronger each time. The fall of the Iron Curtain is a fucking new chapter, our differences can be bridged. Our shared values can prevail, and a more peaceful and prosperous continent can be realized."

Alex chuckled again, a glint of mischief in his eyes. "Ah, my friend, you paint a rosy picture indeed. But tell me, what about the inevitable clashes of national interests? The tensions that arise when different countries vie for resources, influence, and power? Will the European Union truly be able to overcome these challenges?"

Peter leaned back, considering the question. "It won't be easy. Yea, I admit that. But I have faith in the power of dialogue, negotiation, and compromise. The European Union was born out of a desire to prevent the tragedies of the past and build a more harmonious future. It may take time, but I believe the EU will evolve, adapt, and find ways to address the diverse needs and aspirations of its member states."

Alex chuckled again, his laughter rich with a touch of irony. "Ah, my dear Peter, you speak of diplomacy and compromise as if they are simple tasks. The reality is that politics is a messy business. Self-interest often trumps collective aspirations. The European Union would just serving as a mere façade of unity. The Future of Europe would be characterized by competing national agendas"

Peter raised an eyebrow, his tone playful. "Oh, Alex, you're quite the pessimist, aren't you? But isn't it precisely the existence of differing opinions and perspectives that allows for growth and progress? The challenges we face will push us to find innovative solutions, to understand one another better, and to forge a stronger European identity."

Alex chuckled once more, a twinkle in his eye. "Well, Peter, perhaps you're right. After all, life would be dull if we all agreed on everything. Perhaps the future of Europe lies somewhere in between our divergent predictions—a delicate balance of unity and diversity, of cooperation and competition. Only time will tell."

As their laughter subsided, Daniel wished to hear more as he had more questions. The men seem to be out of time and had to be on their way. 'Tori' the little man called to his daughter, who left her flowers and ran to him giggling. The tall man called on his son and they walked off to the car. Alex embraced his daughter, leaving his newspaper behind on the desk. They but followed Peter and walked to their own car.

Daniel looked at the newspaper and picked it up. He unfolded a newspaper, and his eyes were immediately drawn to the bold inscription that adorned the front page: "The Iron Curtain Falls: The Soviet Union Collapses."

A surge of emotions washed over Daniel as he read those words, the significance of the moment sinking in. The news marked the end of an era—an era defined by tension, secrecy, and the constant threat of conflict. The Soviet Union, once a formidable force on the world stage, had crumbled under the weight of its own contradictions and internal strife.

For decades, Daniel had navigated the treacherous landscape of espionage, often battling against the influence and reach of the Soviet Union. He had witnessed firsthand the far-reaching consequences of their machinations, the lives torn apart, and the countless sacrifices made in the name of ideology. And now, here he sat, witnessing the collapse of the very system he had fought against.

A mix of relief, disbelief, and a sense of profound change coursed through Daniel's veins. The fall of the Iron Curtain meant the end of an ideological divide that had shaped his entire life. The world, as he knew it, was undergoing a seismic shift—one that held both promise and uncertainty for the future.

As he delved deeper into the newspaper, Daniel absorbed the details of the momentous event. The article painted a picture of a crumbling empire, the struggles of a nation grappling with economic turmoil, political unrest, and a growing desire for freedom and self-determination. The revelations of corruption, suppression, and the truth behind the propaganda machine began to surface, exposing the hollow foundations on which the Soviet Union had stood.

In the midst of this historic moment, Daniel couldn't help but reflect on his own journey. He had dedicated his life to protecting his country and preserving its values in the face of the communist threat. The battles fought, the lives lost, and the sacrifices made were all part of a larger struggle—one that had ultimately led to this moment of triumph.

As he sat in the park, absorbing the magnitude of the news, Daniel felt a mix of emotions—gratitude for those who had fought alongside him, sadness for the lives lost in the pursuit of freedom, and a sense of accomplishment that his efforts had contributed, in some small way, to this significant turning point in history.

But amidst the celebrations and the sense of victory, Daniel knew that challenges lay ahead. The newspaper stated that things were far from being over as the collapse of the Soviet Union would bring about its own set of complications—a power vacuum, economic instability, and the need to address the wounds of a divided world. It would require not only political acumen but also a collective effort to heal the scars of the past and forge a path toward a more peaceful and prosperous future.

As he closed the newspaper, Daniel took a deep breath, allowing the weight of the moment to settle within him. The world was changing, and he understood that his role in the grand scheme of things had also evolved. The battles he had fought and the secrets he had safeguarded had played a part in dismantling a system that had held the world in its grip.

With the fall of the Iron Curtain, Daniel found himself at a crossroads—a moment of reflection and possibility. He contemplated the path that lay ahead for the little ones. The world is now made a far better place for them. He hopes with all his heart that their innocence is preserved and they have a safe transition into the realities of life and adulthood.

As he stood up from the park bench, Daniel carried with him the newspaper tucked underneath his armpit and walked on. In the bustling streets of London. As he strolled, he couldn't help but notice the abundance of the national flag proudly adorning buildings, lampposts, and shop windows. The familiar hues of red, white, and blue seemed to permeate every corner, filling the air with a palpable sense of celebration.

The atmosphere was infectious, with people of all ages and backgrounds donning clothing and accessories that displayed their love for their country. Faces lit up with smiles, as if the shared recognition of their collective identity had forged an unspoken bond between strangers. The city had transformed into a sea of joy, and Daniel found himself immersed in its currents.

Children ran through the streets, waving miniature flags with unbridled enthusiasm. Their laughter mingled with the sounds of street performers and the cheers of onlookers. Families gathered in parks, engaging in traditional games and activities, their faces radiant with pride and joy. The air resonated with the melodies of patriotic songs, sung by choirs and musicians who filled the city's squares.

The aroma of street food wafted through the air, as vendors served up quintessentially British fare—fish and chips, pies, and scones. The tantalizing scents mingled with the sounds of laughter and conversation, creating a tapestry of sensory delight that made Daniel feel more connected to the city and its people.

Every corner of London seemed to exude a sense of historical significance. Monuments and statues stood tall, embodying the legacy of a nation that had weathered trials and triumphs. The very cobblestones beneath Daniel's feet seemed to echo the footsteps of those who had come before, their struggles and achievements etched into the city's DNA.

The English flag, the iconic St. George's Cross, fluttered proudly in the breeze, adding a splash of color to the urban landscape. From buildings to lamp posts, the flag seemed to be everywhere, as if the city itself had come alive with a sense of national pride.

The people he encountered wore expressions of joy and contentment, their faces brightened by smiles that mirrored the sunny skies above. Many individuals donned clothing in shades of red, white, and blue, proudly displaying their allegiance to their country. Hats, shirts, scarves, and even face paint all bore the familiar hues, creating a visual tapestry of patriotism.

Passing by a park, Daniel witnessed a group of friends engaging in a friendly game of cricket. Their laughter filled the air, punctuated by the satisfying crack of the bat as the ball was hit. Each participant wore a small English flag pinned to their clothing, a symbol of their collective spirit and support for their nation.

Further down the street, he noticed a street performer entertaining a crowd with his captivating act. Wearing a striking outfit adorned with the Union Jack, he juggled colorful balls with impressive skill, drawing applause and cheers from the onlookers. His performance seemed to embody the joyous spirit of the day, as if the celebration of patriotism had permeated every facet of life in the city.

As Daniel continued his walk, he passed by a pub where patrons spilled out onto the sidewalk, their conversations animated and laughter filling the air. The pub's exterior was adorned with large English flags, proudly displayed as a symbol of national identity. He couldn't help but feel the infectious energy and camaraderie that emanated from within, as friends and strangers alike gathered to toast to their shared heritage.

Even the shop windows seemed to participate in the festivities. Decorated with displays featuring English memorabilia, they enticed passersby with a wide array of products and souvenirs that celebrated the country's rich history and cultural heritage. The unmistakable aroma of freshly brewed tea and the sweet scent of scones wafted from nearby cafes, inviting Daniel to take a moment and indulge in these traditional delights.

As he made his way through the streets, Daniel encountered a group of schoolchildren on a field trip, accompanied by their teachers. They walked hand-in-hand, their small flags waving proudly in the breeze. Their young voices resonated with innocence and excitement as they chanted patriotic songs, their enthusiasm infectious and endearing.

The city seemed to radiate with a palpable sense of unity, as everyone present shared a deep connection to their country. Strangers exchanged warm smiles and greetings, acknowledging one another's shared pride. It was a reminder that despite the diverse backgrounds and experiences that made up the fabric of the city, there was a common thread that wove them all together—the love and appreciation for their English heritage.

Daniel found solace amidst the crowd as he walked with purpose towards a quaint flower shop. The warm sunlight filtered through the city's skyline, casting a golden glow upon the cobblestone streets. The sweet fragrance of blossoms wafted through the air, lifting his spirits and invigorating his senses.

As he entered the flower shop, a bell chimed softly, announcing his arrival. The shopkeeper, a friendly-faced woman with silver hair and a warm smile, greeted him with genuine warmth. She had seen him before, a regular customer who often sought refuge in the beauty of nature's creations.

Daniel perused the vibrant displays of blossoms, carefully selecting a bouquet of red poppies. The shopkeeper, sensing the weight of Daniel's intentions, approached the old man with a gentle kindness.

With the bouquet in hand, Daniel thanked the shopkeeper, his eyes reflecting a mixture of gratitude and sadness. He reached into his pocket and pulled out a generous sum of money, placing it gently on the counter as a token of appreciation. The shopkeeper's eyes widened in surprise, a glimmer of gratitude shining through her gaze. It was a small act of kindness, a gesture to express his appreciation for her understanding and the beauty she curated within her humble store.

Leaving the flower shop behind, Daniel set forth towards a public graveyard, his steps measured and purposeful. The atmosphere shifted as he entered the solemn realm of the resting place, the gentle whispers of the wind carrying a sense of reverence. The air seemed to grow still, as if nature itself recognized the significance of this moment.

His heart heavy with memories, Daniel found himself standing before a modest tombstone, adorned only with a simple inscription: **Gilla**.

Kneeling before the grave, Daniel delicately placed the bouquet upon the freshly trimmed grass. The flowers, vibrant and alive, stood in stark contrast to the muted surroundings. He got up, took of her hat, bowed his head and closed his eyes. He whispered a prayer softly on his lips, as he sought solace and closure in this quiet sanctuary.

Memories of Gilla flooded his mind—her strength, her vulnerability, and the choices she had made in the name of a greater cause. He reflected on their encounters, the twists and turns of their shared journey, and the truths that had been unearthed. Gilla's presence lingered in his thoughts,

As Daniel stood by the grave, he allowed himself to feel the weight of his emotions. Grief intertwined with gratitude, sadness mingled with a deep sense of admiration. He acknowledged the impact Gilla had made on his life and the lives of others, a beacon of resilience and sacrifice in a world filled with shadows.

As Daniel knelt by Gilla's grave, a flood of emotions surged through his being. The weight of the past and the memories of those he had lost consumed his thoughts. In that solemn moment, his mind was drawn to two women whose lives had intersected with his in profound and devastating ways—Mary and Gilla.

Mary, his beloved secretary, had been a pillar of strength and support throughout their years together. Her unwavering love and understanding had sustained him during the darkest of times. He remembered her warm smile, the gentle touch of her hand, and the laughter they had shared in moments of respite from their perilous lives. She had been his anchor, his sanctuary amidst the chaos that surrounded them.

Gilla, on the other hand, was the complex figure who had captivated and perplexed him. She had been both ally and adversary, a woman shrouded in mystery and driven by her own convictions. The revelation of her past had shattered the assumptions he had held about her. But Gilla's death had left an indelible mark on his soul.

As Daniel sat by Gilla's grave, the weight of loss and the realization of the forces at play in their lives overwhelmed him. Tears welled in his eyes, and a profound sadness washed over him. It was not a mourning for the physical absence of Mary and Gilla but a lamentation for the higher powers and political machinations that had conspired to manipulate and exploit their lives.

In the world of espionage, loyalty and betrayal were often intertwined, obscured by the murky depths of power and ideology. Daniel had witnessed firsthand the manipulations, the sacrifices, and the collateral damage that accompanied the pursuit of greater causes. Mary and Gilla had become casualties of a game played by those who wielded influence from the shadows—a game in which the lives of individuals were mere pawns in a grander scheme.

His tears were a testament to the profound injustice that pervaded their lives, a lament for the innocent souls caught in the crossfire of political machinations. He wept not only for Mary and Gilla but for the countless others whose stories had been erased or distorted by the whims of those in power. Their deaths were not just tragedies but reminders of the inherent dangers that lurked within the world of espionage.

In his grief, Daniel recalled the realization that the very system he had dedicated his life to protecting was riddled with corruption and manipulation. The higher powers and political forces that had orchestrated Mary and Gilla's demise were faceless entities, elusive and immune to the consequences of their actions.

Soon, as Daniel sat alone in the quiet solitude of the public graveyard, he couldn't help but feel a sense of peace enveloping him. The somber atmosphere of the place seemed to whisper stories of the departed, their sorrows, and their triumphs. The gentle rustling of leaves and the distant chirping of birds created a serene backdrop, amplifying the tranquility that Daniel longed for.

As he looked around, his gaze fell upon the rows of gravestones. But amidst the weight of his emotions that moment, Daniel began to feel a subtle shift within him. It was as if the graveyard itself held a secret, a key to unlocking the shackles of guilt and regret that had bound him for years. The air felt lighter, as if forgiveness was swirling around him, waiting to be embraced.

He closed his eyes and took a deep breath, allowing the crisp, cool air to fill his lungs. With each exhale, he released the remnants of his past, surrendering to the healing power of the present moment. The weight on his shoulders gradually lifted, replaced by a newfound sense of liberation.

In this sacred space, Daniel found solace in the belief that forgiveness is not only granted by others but also by oneself. He acknowledged his flaws, his mistakes, and the pain he had caused.

In this act of reverence and introspection, Daniel felt a profound release. The burdens that had weighed him down for so long began to dissipate, replaced by a sense of redemption and renewal. He knew that he could not change the past, but he could choose how he carried it within him.

As he stood up and started his walk through the graveyard, he noticed the sunlight filtering through the branches, casting gentle rays of warmth upon the tombstones. The beauty of the moment filled his heart with a renewed appreciation for life, for the resilience of the human spirit, and for the power of forgiveness.

With each step, Daniel embraced the freedom that forgiveness offered. He knew that moving forward would not be without challenges, but he felt equipped with a newfound strength and resilience.

In the quiet corners of the graveyard, Daniel found closure. He had released the shackles of guilt, redeemed himself in his own eyes, and found forgiveness amidst the whispers of the departed. With a heart full of gratitude and a spirit renewed, Daniel wandered through the hallowed grounds of the graveyard like a happy child. It was a gratitude that transcended the boundaries of life and death, intertwining the beauty and fragility of existence in a delicate dance.

The air felt charged with a sacred energy, carrying the whispers of souls who had departed from this earthly realm. Daniel found himself drawn to the quietude of the place, as if the serenity of the graveyard invited introspection and reflection. He marveled at the myriad stories buried beneath the earth, the layers of human experience etched into each tombstone.

The stillness embraced him, allowing his thoughts to settle and his heart to open. In this space of contemplation, he found himself overcome by a profound gratitude for the gift of life. It was as if every breath he took was infused with the awareness of the sheer miracle of existence, the intricate tapestry of emotions, sensations, and connections that make up a human life.

He closed his eyes, letting the sunlight filter through his eyelids, casting a warm, golden hue upon his face. The sensation evoked a deep appreciation for the vibrant colors of the world, for the way nature painted masterpieces with each changing season. The gentle caress of the breeze upon his skin reminded him of the delicate balance between fragility and strength, the interplay of vulnerability and resilience that defines our human journey.

In this moment of reflection, Daniel's gratitude extended beyond the realm of the living. He began to recognize the beauty and purpose of death, the way it weaves its presence into the fabric of existence. The tombstones, adorned with flowers and tokens of remembrance, served as poignant reminders of the lives that had touched others, the legacies that had left indelible imprints upon the world.

He walked among the graves, reading the names and dates etched into the stone. Each one represented a unique story, a life that had left its mark, however fleeting or profound. It was a humbling reminder of the interconnectedness of all beings, the intricate web of lives intersecting and influencing one another in ways both seen and unseen.

As Daniel continued his journey, he felt a deep appreciation for the lessons he had learned, the relationships he had forged, and the experiences that had shaped him into the person he had become. Even the moments of struggle and pain held a place in his heart, for they had sculpted his character, teaching him resilience, compassion, and empathy.

His gratitude extended to the people who had walked alongside him on his path, the friends and loved ones who had offered support, love, and understanding. Their presence, like rays of sunlight on a cloudy day, had illuminated his life and provided solace in times of darkness. In their embrace, he had discovered the true meaning of connection and belonging.

With each step, Daniel felt a profound sense of gratitude for the fleeting nature of time. It reminded him to savor every precious moment, to cherish the simple joys, and to embrace the full spectrum of human emotions. Life, he realized, is a delicate dance of light and shadow, and it is in the acknowledgement of both that we find depth and meaning.

As he made his way toward the exit of the graveyard, a profound stillness settled within him. The weight of his worries and regrets had lifted, replaced by a profound appreciation for the tapestry of life and death that unfolded before his eyes. He left the graveyard with a heart overflowing with gratitude, a renewed sense of purpose, and a profound reverence for the beauty of existence.

The world outside the graveyard seemed to sparkle with newfound clarity. The colors appeared more vibrant, the sounds more melodic, and the fragrances more intoxicating. Daniel embraced each moment with a sense of wonder and joy.

THE END

Printed in Great Britain
by Amazon